Words of Praise for

♦ Harlequin®

SPECIAL EDITION

from *New York Times* and *USA TODAY* bestselling authors

"When I started writing for Special Edition,
I was delighted by the length of the books,
which allowed the freedom to create,
and develop more within each character and
their romance. I have always been a fan of
Special Edition! I hope to write for it for many years
to come. Long live Special Edition!
—Diana Palmer

"My career began in Special Edition.
I remember my excitement when the SEs
were introduced, because the stories were so rich and
different, and every month when the books came out
I beat a path to the bookstore to get every one of them. Here's
to you, SE; live long, and prosper!"
—Linda Howard

"Congratulations, Special Edition,
on thirty years of publishing first-class romance!"
—Linda Lael Miller

HAVING ADAM'S BABY

CHRISTYNE BUTLER

Harlequin

SPECIAL EDITION

ISBN-13: 978-0-373-65664-6

HAVING ADAM'S BABY

Copyright © 2012 by Christyne Butilier

THE ANNIVERSARY PARTY
Copyright © 2012 by Harlequin Books S.A.

The publisher acknowledges the following writers who contributed to THE ANNIVERSARY PARTY: RaeAnne Thayne, Christine Rimmer, Susan Crosby, Christyne Butler, Gina Wilkins and Cindy Kirk.

Recycling programs
for this product may
not exist in your area.

www.Harlequin.com

Printed in U.S.A.

CONTENTS

Books by Christyne Butler

Harlequin Special Edition

Fortune's Secret Baby #2114
*Welcome Home, Bobby Winslow #2145
*Having Adam's Baby #2182

Silhouette Special Edition

*The Cowboy's Second Chance #1980
*The Sheriff's Secret Wife #2022
*A Daddy for Jacoby #2089

Harlequin Books

Special Edition Bonus Story:
The Anniversary Party—Chapter Four

*Welcome to Destiny
†The Fortunes of Texas: Lost…and Found

Other titles by this author available in ebook format.

CHRISTYNE BUTLER

fell in love with romance novels while serving in the United States Navy and started writing her own stories six years ago. She considers selling to Harlequin Special Edition a dream come true and enjoys writing contemporary romances full of life, love, a hint of laughter and perhaps a dash of danger, too. And there has to be a happily-ever-after or she's just not satisfied.

She lives with her family in central Massachusetts and loves to hear from her readers at chris@christynebutler.com. Or visit her website at www.christynebutler.com.

Dear Reader,

Where were you in '82? I was busy with the junior prom, falling in love for the first time and hanging out with my friends. What was Harlequin doing? Introducing a "special" line of romances to its family! The first Harlequin books I read were Special Edition titles, and I am so honored to be part of their 30th anniversary celebration.

I am also very excited to introduce you all to a new family in my Welcome to Destiny series—the Murphys! Two of the brothers made appearances in earlier books, but now the entire family, three generations who live and love while running the family business, Murphy Mountain Log Homes, is here!

Becoming a parent can be both the scariest and most exciting time in a person's life and while Adam Murphy and Fay Coggen have a complicated history that makes finding their own happily-ever-after a bit tougher, it's also so worth it! Please email me at chris@christynebutler.com and let me know if you enjoyed Adam and Fay's story and stay tuned for more stories featuring Adam's brothers!

Christyne

To the men and woman who have served proudly
in our Armed Forces,
most especially my father,
Staff Sergeant Kenneth D. Toms, USAF, Retired.
Miss you every day, Dad!

HAVING ADAM'S BABY

Chapter One

Fay Coggen was sick and tired of being sick and tired.

Eating healthier would help. More tofu-laced salads, less Chinese takeout. Her thirty-five-year-old body would thank her later. The heavy lifting required at her florist shop toned her arms and shoulders, but her backside would be better served if she did more at night than read or work on crossword puzzles, two favorite pastimes that kept her butt planted firmly on the couch.

Getting a decent night's sleep would probably work wonders, too. After eighteen months, she still wasn't used to sleeping alone. Even though she'd been on her own for longer than that, in more ways than she could count.

Still, more rest would help her kick this nagging cold she'd had for the last two months. With the busy Fourth of July holiday and the one-year anniversary of Scott's death just a few weeks away, she needed all the energy she could get.

All reasons why she was sitting in her doctor's office on this sunny June afternoon.

As far as medical facilities went, this one was pretty nice. Pale-yellow-and-white gingham wallpaper covered three walls. The fourth boasted a large bay window that looked out onto a lush lawn, stately rows of green hedges and a wooden bench surrounded by a carpet of red and purple impatiens beneath a shady tree.

And despite the fact she and Liz were friends, Fay could honestly say she'd hated every moment she'd spent here.

"So sorry to have kept you waiting." Liz's lilting voice filled the air as she hustled into the room and closed the door behind her. "I wanted to double-check the test results myself."

Her friend sat in the matching chair across from Fay, instead of taking her seat behind her desk. Fay smiled. "Over a simple case of the flu? Things must be pretty slow around here. So what are the doctor's orders? Lots of rest and orange juice?"

Liz crossed one ankle over the other with a natural grace. "We haven't had a chance to visit in a while. How are you feeling, Fay?"

"Other than wishing for a week where I could do nothing but sleep, I'm fine. Like I told your nurse, the dizziness comes and goes, and it'd be nice to eat something more substantial than soup and crackers. The news predicted a terrible flu season that would carry on into spring. They weren't kidding."

"I'm talking about how you're doing emotionally."

The older woman glanced pointedly at Fay's lap. "I notice you haven't gone back to wearing your wedding rings."

Fay clenched her battle-scarred florist hands, her thumb and forefinger automatically rubbing at the indentation on her left hand that was almost gone. "I told you that I decided to take them off back around Christmas."

"Understandable. Scott had been gone for six months by then."

Understandable after she'd discovered the lies and secrets her late husband had left in the wake of his death last summer. After fifteen years of marriage, she'd thought neither of them had the ability to surprise each other anymore.

She'd been wrong and trying to recover ever since.

"You said you were wearing them on a chain around your neck instead." Liz's gaze moved over the open collar of Fay's blouse. "I see that's gone now, too."

Yes, the chain and her rings were buried in the bottom of her jewelry box, along with her husband's dog tags.

Ever since that night two months ago.

Ever since Adam Murphy.

"Are you involved with anyone?" Liz asked.

"What?" Her friend's question jolted Fay from her thoughts. "No, of course not. Just because I decided— That doesn't mean I'm—" Fay realized she was babbling and paused, fought for a controlled breath and then continued. "Dating isn't something I'm even thinking about."

"I know things have been difficult, but it's okay to

move on. Next month will make it a year since Scott died. Finding someone new to spend time with, maybe even thinking about falling—"

"Liz, between trying to hold on to my business and sorting out the colossal mess Scott's creative financing left me, my life's been nothing but chaos for the last year. Believe me, I'm working hard at moving on."

"I meant with a man."

Fay let loose a bark of laughter that wasn't close to being humorous. "I know what you meant, but no."

"Sweetie, then this is going to be a shock." Liz placed the folder she was holding in her lap and reached out, laying a comforting hand on her arm. "You don't have the flu. You're pregnant."

Her friend's words echoed in Fay's ears, each time becoming more muted and garbled.

She hadn't heard her friend correctly.

There was no way she'd heard correctly.

"You must be wrong." Fay shook her head. "I only have one working ovary, remember? An ovary that works at a reduced capacity making it impossible for me to get preg—" She bit off the word, unable to say it aloud. "You said so yourself."

"I told you years ago that pregnancy was improbable, especially when Scott refused to have any testing done. As you know, your inability to conceive for all those years could have been just as much him." Liz tightened her fingers in a gentle squeeze. "The test results are positive. You are pregnant."

A baby. After years of wanting, desperately wanting a child and now…

"We can discuss your options. Out of the office if that would be better."

Fay's hands automatically flattened low over her belly. "Options?"

"You just said you aren't involved with anyone. Did something…happen?"

"Something?"

Liz's gaze filled with concern. "Honey, were you hurt or forced—"

"No, no, of course not." Fay's protest came swiftly, just like the eight-week-old memories from those passion-filled, guilt-ridden hours spent in Adam's arms. "I was— I mean, it was unplanned and impulsive, but I knew what I was doing."

Yes, she certainly had.

Sleeping with her dead husband's best friend, someone who was once her good friend as well, was the real reason Fay no longer wore her rings.

Not after the way she'd straddled Adam's lap and helped him yank her sweater over her head. Eagerness had her bracing her hands on his wide shoulders, leaning forward to take his mouth again only to have the twin gold bands, one with a marquise-shaped diamond, dangle between them.

They'd brushed against Adam's jaw and he'd fisted them, asking in that deep, guttural tone of his if she was sure about what they were doing.

If she knew who she was with.

You, Adam. I want you.

A heated blush raced up Fay's neck until it reached her cheeks. The memory of that night, and the way she'd run out on him the next morning after learning

Adam was heading back overseas, back to his Air Force reserve unit, the same unit her husband had served with until his death, was as fresh and real as if it had happened only last night.

Of course, in her dreams it had.

"This is a shock, I realize that." Liz offered a warm smile, her words forcing Fay to push away the memories. "Take your time to think about your next step."

"I'm having this baby."

The words were soft, but spoken with a sense of purpose Fay hadn't felt in a long time. No hesitation, no question about right or wrong, no reason for her to think about this at all.

She squared her shoulders and righted her posture. "I want this—my baby. I'm keeping my baby."

"And the father?"

A wave of dizziness washed over her. Fay swallowed hard to maintain her equilibrium as her heart pounded in her chest and a rush of heat again stole over her body.

Adam Murphy was due to return to Destiny from his last tour in Afghanistan in a couple of weeks. How was she going to tell the man she blamed for her husband's death he was going to be the father of her child?

"Hey, soldier, don't I know you from somewhere?"

Master Sergeant Adam Murphy squared his shoulders and stood a bit taller, but he didn't turn around.

He knew that voice.

There were only six possible people it could belong to. People who, according to his mother, all shared the same low masculine growl that could soothe a skittish horse or sweet-talk a girl out of her better judgment.

It had to be one of his five younger brothers or their dad.

Which one had spotted him standing here, in front of the beer cooler at a convenience mart on the outskirts of Cheyenne of all places, he didn't know. He hoped it was Devlin, the brother he was closest to despite there being one other between them in ages. Or maybe it was Ric, the youngest, whom Adam had bossed around like a second father. He'd been fourteen when the kid was born.

Geez, he felt old.

He turned, bracing himself, and found Dev grinning at him.

"Hey, bro."

"What the hell are you doing here?" Adam asked.

"Shouldn't I be asking you that question?"

Dev lunged, pulling him into a bear hug that Adam returned with ease. He blinked hard against the sudden sting in his eyes, giving his brother a few extra hardy thumps to the back before they broke apart.

"Damn, it's good to see you," Dev said. "What are you doing in Cheyenne? You weren't due back from Afghanistan for another ten days or so."

"The entire unit is coming back sooner than scheduled, in less than a week, but I was able to catch an earlier ride home."

Dev arched one eyebrow. "And you didn't bother to let anyone in the family know?"

"It was last-minute, and I could've gotten bumped off the flight anywhere along the way." Adam had hoped to slip back into town without anyone finding out. He didn't want to explain how he'd finagled avoiding the pageantry of his unit's arrival at the air base after being overseas for the past year and a half. "The plane finally landed at Camp Guernsey a few hours ago. I caught a ride with a retired vet who was heading toward Destiny."

His brother peered around Adam's shoulder at the rows of ice-cold beers in the refrigerated unit behind him. "And the two of you decided to stop and pick up a few brews?"

"He decided," Adam said. "I was just admiring the view."

Dev smiled and seconds later had a twelve-pack tucked under his arm. "Come on, I think you've earned this."

"You sure?" Dev had walked away from booze years ago after finally admitting his nightly partying led to nothing but sleepovers at the local jail and finally AA meetings. Adam didn't want to tempt him.

"Hey, this is all for you, bro." Dev offered an easy smile. "Come on, let's find your Good Samaritan and let him know you've got a new taxi service."

Knowing it was useless to argue with a Murphy, Adam only nodded. He thanked the old man as he pulled his duffel from the back of his pickup and tossed it into his brother's Jeep.

The ride home took almost an hour and Adam was grateful when Dev used that time to do what he did best. Talk. He jumped from subject to subject, mostly getting Adam caught up on all he'd missed while serving his last tour.

Yes, he'd been home two months ago, once again as an escort bringing home a deceased member of his command at the request of a grieving family in

Cheyenne. He'd managed to add two days in Destiny, long enough to share a couple of meals with the family.

And an amazing night with the one woman he'd always wanted.

And could never have.

But he did have her. And she'd had him. For a few incredible hours on a makeshift bed in his living room in front of a blazing fire. They'd had each other.

Adam turned to the window, closed his eyes and inhaled sharply, certain he could still smell the clean, flowery scent that always surrounded Fay.

He'd answered the pounding on his front door that rainy night, wearing nothing but hastily buttoned jeans and a bemused expression.

Fay had stormed into his living room, hair and clothes damp. Shocked that she'd known he was in town, he'd only stood there and listened as she ranted and raved, releasing all her anger and grief as she blamed him for her husband's death the previous summer.

He'd escorted Scott's body home and stayed for the services, but he and Fay had hardly spoken to each other that hot July day. She'd certainly made up for the lapse that night, but hell, she didn't say anything to him that he hadn't been telling himself.

So he let her talk. But Fay had worked herself into a frenzy while she paced, not paying attention to what she was doing or where she was walking. When she tripped over his duffel bag, he'd reached out and caught her, pulling her hard to his chest. Off balance, they fell together onto the couch.

Her words disappeared, leaving only choppy breaths

that had torched his bare skin like fire. Her fingertips pressed against his chest and not kissing her had been damn near impossible—

"Hey, bro. You okay?"

Adam jerked his head around.

Blinking away the memories, he forced words past the hard lump in his throat. "What? Yeah, I'm fine."

"You're looking a bit pasty." Dev turned his attention from the road to look at him. "What are you thinking about?"

Shaking his head, Adam noticed they'd already driven through the center of Destiny, right past Fay's shop, and he hadn't even noticed.

He yanked his BDU—Battle Dress Uniform—cap farther down over his forehead. "Nothing. Go on, keep talking."

Dev rattled on about the family business, Murphy Mountain Log Homes, and how well things were going even in the current uncertain economic times.

Designing and building a log mansion for local racing champion Bobby Winslow last year had brought in a slew of new customers from all over the country, each with money to spend on their dream home.

Like his parents and five brothers, Adam was a part owner, but much to his father's dismay he'd walked away from any involvement in the day-to-day running of the business years ago, leaving his younger brothers to fill key management roles.

"Is it too soon to bug you about your plans?" Devlin asked.

"Sleep."

"I mean now that you're home. For good. You're still set to retire, right?"

Adam nodded. He'd recently completed twenty years in the Air Force reserves, most of the last four years spent more soldier than civilian. Thanks to the unused leave time he'd accumulated he was essentially out of the military with his official retirement set to take place in a few months.

He was ready to return to his first love, ranching.

Right after college he'd purchased a share of the family's holdings from his father with the dream of raising horses and cattle. But other than building his log home, life had gotten in the way of his plans. Now, it was time to make that dream a reality by putting the pastures and the section of the Blue Creek River that cut through his land to good use.

Devlin slowed at a crossroads. A right turn would lead them to the family compound and company headquarters. He looked at Adam and offered an arched brow as if he already knew what the answer would be.

Adam pointed left. "I've been up almost twenty-four hours straight. I need sack time more than anything else right now."

His brother steered them down the road to Adam's place. The closer they got, the more restless he grew to see his home again. He rolled down the window, letting a cool summer breeze wash over him. It'd been blisteringly hot in Afghanistan when he'd boarded the military transport, but here in Destiny, tucked up against the foothills of the Laramie Mountains, it was a perfect day with lots of sunshine, green trees and the fresh, earthy scent of the great outdoors.

This return was different.

This time he was home for good.

All he wanted was the chance to start his life over again. Alone. Nothing to concentrate on but his land. He was sure his father would try to get him involved in the family business again and his mother would drop hints about wanting her eldest settled with a nice girl.

Been there, done that, and Adam still had the battle scars to prove marriage, kids and a nine-to-five job weren't for him. Spending as much time alone working on his ranch was the perfect plan.

At some point, he'd have to find a way to make things right with Fay, but there wasn't any rush. Destiny wasn't a big town, but he could keep out of her way, positive she wasn't in any hurry to spend time with him.

Not after the way she'd torn out of his place when she'd awakened to find him dressed in his uniform ready to head back overseas.

No, Fay Coggen had made it perfectly clear two months ago she wanted nothing more to do with him.

He may not like it, but he'd learn to live with it.

Devlin pulled into the driveway and cut the engine.

Realizing his brother planned to come inside, Adam sighed and punched in the code on his cell phone to deactivate his home's security system. "I should warn you, the place is probably a mess."

He couldn't remember if he'd washed up the dirty dishes from his visit or even taken out the trash, but for certain the nest of blankets and pillows he and Fay had made love on were still strewn across his living room floor.

Dev joined him on the covered porch that ran the entire circumference of his log home, the twelve-pack of Guinness balanced in the crook of his arm, and rolled his eyes. "Yeah, I'd forgotten how much of a dump the old homestead is."

Retrieving a spare key from behind a bench, Adam paused and looked out over his front yard. The large area thrived with clusters of cottonwoods, freshly mowed grass and trimmed bushes. A recently mulched area with brightly colored flowers was new.

He figured he had his family to thank for that and for the upkeep. A nearby barn and horse corral could use some work, and beyond that lay a hundred and eighty acres ready for hay meadows, horses and cattle-grazing.

"I'm talking about inside my place, moron." Adam dropped his duffel to the floor. "It's going to need airing out if nothing else. I left in a rush."

Dev leaned over and grabbed the bag. "It's a good thing the folks are still trolling around the Southwest in their RV. There'd be hell to pay if they knew you were home and hiding from everyone."

"I need some downtime." Adam opened the door and stepped inside. "A day or two by myself before... What the hell?"

Dev sidestepped behind him. "Whoa, don't want to drop the cargo."

Adam looked around.

Bright sunshine spilled through squeaky-clean windows, filling the large dining and living room with light. Tabletops gleamed and a lemony scent lingered in the air. The area in front of the fireplace held nothing but the Navajo-print rug and the oversize furniture that had been rearranged to allow better viewing of both the flat screen television and the fireplace.

No sign of his and Fay's impromptu bed.

Adam walked in farther and a quick glance at his kitchen revealed that the appliances and countertops shined as if they'd never been used. The dining table, once covered with stacks of laundry, now held only a potted plant—one still alive, at that—and a neat pile of mail.

His place was spotless.

"Looks like your fairy godmother knew you were coming." Dev walked into the kitchen and placed the beer in the refrigerator. "Geez, you've even got orange juice and tubs of butter in here."

Adam shook his head. "Who could've done this?"

"Are you kidding?" Dev tossed a beer at him, then opened a bottled water for himself. "This has Mom written all over it."

Adam easily caught the bottle one-handed, then set it on the table behind the couch. "I talked to Mom a few days ago. She never said anything. Do you think it could be one of the guys or Laurie?"

"Laurie's been busy crunching the numbers for a hot new account." Dev headed for the couch. "Mom did a good job making sure we boys all knew how to cook a hot dog and wash dishes, but clean like this? Forget it."

Adam headed down the hall as his brother continued to ramble. He peeked into the two spare bedrooms, pausing for a long moment in the doorway of the smallest one, still empty except for the gleaming hardwood floor, before walking into his own room.

His king-size bed looked like something out of a

hotel, the blankets neatly tucked and folded and his pillows propped against the hand-hewn timber headboard. A quick stop in the master bathroom showed him the same meticulous care had been taken in there as well.

Peeling off his cap and outer camouflage shirt, he tossed both onto a nearby chair. Hands braced on his hips, he pulled in a few deep breaths, enjoying the silence as finally being home sunk in.

Gone was the constant noise of construction vehicles, twelve-hour workdays and the dust that covered everything at Bagram Airfield.

It wasn't even fifteen hundred—three o'clock in the civilian world—and Adam wanted nothing more than to darken the blinds and dive headfirst into bed. He turned instead and headed back to the main living area.

Grabbing the beer he'd left behind, he joined his brother on the couch.

"Boy, you suddenly look like you've been to hell and back," Dev said. "Fitting, I guess."

Adam sank into the cushions, leaned back and closed his eyes. "Yeah, I guess."

He'd been certain memories of his time in the sandbox would be crowding his head even though he was finally stateside, much like he'd relived that night he'd spent with Fay over and over again while lying in his bunk in Afghanistan.

But they weren't.

Despite his earlier resolve not to dwell on Fay, now that he was back in his own home, all he could think about was what had happened right here eight weeks ago.

Him and Fay. Together.

Finally.

He'd been head over heels for the tiny brunette with long curly hair the moment he'd literally run into her, years ago in the hallways of Destiny High School.

She'd laughed as he lay sprawled at her feet. Two years younger, Fay had been new in town. He'd given the pretty sophomore a quick tour of the building that ended at the school gym, where they'd run into Scott.

And just like that, Adam had faded into the background.

His best friend, and the star quarterback, Scott Coggen had latched his sights on Fay and the rest was history. By the time he and Scott were juniors at the University of Wyoming, Fay was sporting a diamond on her left hand.

Adam felt the beer being lifted from his fingers. He jerked upright, his hand tightening as his eyes flew open. "Hey!"

"Easy, bro." Dev released the bottle and held up both hands in surrender. "Just trying to save a spill. I thought you'd fallen asleep on me."

Had he? Adam honestly didn't know. "Sorry. Maybe I did."

"Look, I'm going to head out and let you get comatose for a while." His brother backed up to the front door. "The folks are due back the day after tomorrow. You plan to be at the house to welcome them home?"

Adam nodded, pushing himself to his feet, his legs like dead weights. "Yeah, I'll be there. And thanks for keeping my return to yourself for now. One Murphy brother is about all I can handle at the moment."

"Considering I'm your favorite, I'll keep your secret." Dev grinned. "Give me a call if you need anything."

A smile creased Adam's face. "Thanks, I will."

After Dev left, Adam poured out his untouched beer, grabbed a water bottle instead and punched in the code on his security system. Minutes later, he stripped down and crawled between the crisp, cool sheets and buried his face in a pillow that smelled like sweet lavender.

Smelled like Fay.

It was his last conscious thought before he fell into a deep, dreamless sleep. He woke up once, the room dark and the clock on his nightstand flashing 2:49 a.m. The next time he cracked an eyelid, the sun was inching around the edges of the window blinds.

Wow, almost ten in the morning. He'd slept over eighteen hours.

Sitting up, he stretched his neck and back while listening to his thirty-eight-year-old body creak and moan as he slowly came to life.

A shower. Lingering beneath the hot spray of his own shower sounded like a slice of heaven. Adam reached into the closest dresser drawer and pulled out a clean T-shirt, jeans and briefs.

Entering the bathroom, he eyed the large whirlpool tub, realizing for the first time he'd never used it in all the years he'd lived here. Tempting, but chances were he'd fall back asleep and probably drown in the process.

Minutes later he stood, hands braced against the tile wall as hot water pounded his neck and shoulders, washing away the soapy residue. Steam filled the glass enclosure and he breathed deeply, pulling the moist air into his lungs and letting it seep into every pore.

When the water cooled, he turned it off and stepped out. Grabbing a nearby towel, he quickly dried, pausing when he heard a low-pitched creaking. He listened intently, but only silence filled the house. After walking naked back into his bedroom, he pulled on his briefs and heard the creak again.

No, that was footsteps.

It had to be Devlin. He was the only one who could override the security system. Exasperation surged inside him. Hadn't he made it clear he wanted to be left alone?

"Oh, shoot! Come on, please cooperate."

The words carried down the hall from the main room. Someone was in his house. A female someone.

The sound of an object shattering and a high-pitched cry had Adam racing down the hall. He entered the living room and found a woman, bent at the waist and clutching one of the stools at the kitchen counter. By her feet lay the remains of a large plant, its bright green leaves and pieces of the broken ceramic pot scattered across the floor.

His anger disappeared and concern took its place. "Hey, are you okay?"

The woman jerked upright and spun around.

Adam stared, the blow to the gut more powerful than any physical contact. Was she a figment of his imagination?

He blinked hard to erase her image. Nope, she still stood less than three feet away from him.

Golden brown curls, pulled back in a messy ponytail, whipped against one cheek. Dark smudges beneath her wide hazel eyes spoke of sleepless nights. She wore a pale green T-shirt with Fay's Flowers printed across her curves and jean shorts that showed off miles of leg.

One hand pressed against her stomach and as her eyes widened at the sight of him, her other hand quickly covered the first.

Just as beautiful as he remembered.

"Fay."

Her skin paled even more the moment he spoke her name.

"What—" Adam voice caught and damn if he didn't have to start again. "What are you doing here?"

Chapter Two

Fay's lips parted and the breath fled from her lungs. Shock battered her insides like stinging pin pricks at the sight before her.

Adam.

He stood spotlighted in a beam of bright sun, all toned muscles and tanned skin, except for the dark blue boxer briefs that hugged him in all the best huggable places.

The man was nearly naked.

What had he asked her? It had been a simple question, one she should be able to answer, but a now familiar rippling of her stomach had her slapping one hand over her mouth. She bolted past him and disappeared into the hall bathroom.

Keeping her eyes screwed tightly shut, her body retaliated, as it had for the last few mornings since her visit to Liz's office, and emptied itself of her breakfast.

The one meal of the day that had always been her favorite.

Not anymore. No matter what she ate, from fruit to cereal to eggs, nothing had staying power. She'd hoped the fresh watermelon she'd eaten an hour ago would be the answer.

She'd been wrong.

"Are you okay?"

Adam's voice, soft but clear, made her jump. He'd followed her and stood close. Very close. Her fingers tightened where she gripped the toilet seat. Of all the humiliating moments in a woman's life, this had to be the worst.

"No." She cringed at the hoarseness of her voice.

"Can I get you anything?"

Fay opened her eyes, averting her gaze to the white floor tiles and found one masculine leg in her line of sight. All she could see was from his knee down, but the naturally tanned skin covered with fine hair instantly brought back the full-body image from moments ago when he'd suddenly appeared in his living room.

How was it her body could go from sickness to hunger within the span of a few seconds?

Hormones, hormones, hormones.

Thanks to the "what to expect" book Fay had bought recently, she'd latched on to the most popular reason for all the craziness her body was going through. Blamed for everything from morning sickness to her breasts suddenly being a tad too big for her bras, hormones had to be the reason her first thought at the sight of Adam had been—

"Fay?"

His voice had her stomach flipping over again. "Privacy. I need privacy."

He stepped back into the hall and she stretched out one leg and kicked the door closed. Curling her feet back beneath her backside and still too weak to move—and not completely sure yet if she should—Fay grabbed a nearby hand towel and wiped at her mouth.

She settled for leaning against the cool porcelain of the bathtub, one hand pressed gently to her stomach.

Adam was home.

So much for one more week to finish the work on his home and to find a way to tell him he was going to be a father.

How could she tell him about the baby?

Soon the changes in her body would be visible—to him, to everyone—and it wouldn't take Adam long to figure out when she'd gotten pregnant. Not that she'd even think of passing this child off as anyone else's.

No, this baby was his, and despite all the lunacy her body was going through, she was already so in love with their child. After giving up any hope of experiencing this kind of miracle herself, she planned to enjoy every minute.

Even the not-so-pleasant ones like this.

A quick knock on the door sent Fay's heart racing. She wasn't ready yet. Adam had returned earlier than scheduled and she needed more time. Time to think, to plan, to figure what she was going to do about her business, the apartment, her in-laws, her parents…

About him.

The door opened, but only Adam's hand appeared, a large glass of ice water in his grasp. He set it down on the sink and retreated, but then a sealed toothbrush and small tube of toothpaste joined the glass.

The door closed again with a quiet click and Fay released the breath she wasn't even aware she'd been holding.

The nausea mostly gone, she rose and quickly rinsed out her mouth, brushed her teeth and splashed water on her face. Her reflection in the mirror had her yanking out her ponytail and redoing it, trying to tame her curls in a messy knot on top of her head.

She drank the ice water, its coolness bathing her throat as she strained to hear anything on the other side of the door.

Was he still there?

Of course he was still here. He lived here. And he had every right to know why she was in his home, breaking dishes and tossing her cookies in his bathroom.

She took a deep breath and threw back her shoulders to fake confidence she wished she felt. If only she knew what to say when she walked back into the living room.

She opened the door and froze.

Adam leaned casually against the far wall, all six feet plus of him, arms crossed over his naked chest, bare feet crossed at his ankles. At least he'd pulled on a pair of jeans, even if they did ride low enough on his hips for those dark briefs to peek out over the waistband.

Her stomach clenched again. Tingling sensations danced over her skin from head to toe, and her throat went dry.

This she couldn't blame on the pregnancy.

No, the blame was squarely on him. The reaction echoed those uncontrollable feelings the night she'd landed in his arms. Instead of continuing to rant against what his advice to his best friend had cost her, she had given in as he'd lowered his mouth and gently brushed his lips over hers.

Then she'd kissed him back.

"You feeling better?"

Fay's gaze jerked to his face, and she realized he'd been watching her gawk. She swallowed hard and forced herself to move past him as she replied, "Yes, thank you."

"Was it something you ate?"

"No."

"Was it the sight of me?"

Her footsteps faltered at his question. "N-no, of course not."

"So what?" Adam pushed, following her. "Some sort of bug or the flu?"

Yes, the nine-month flu, only she prayed the books were right and this awful morning sickness would ease after the first trimester.

"I'm just…not feeling well." Back in the dining area, Fay saw he hadn't cleaned up her mess. Thankful for the excuse, she knelt down and started gathering the broken fronds of the potted fern. "Sorry about this. I'll get this picked up—"

"Fay, what's going on?" Adam moved to stand directly in front of her. "What are *you* doing here?"

"Get back, there are sharp pieces here and you're barefoot." She brushed at his jean-clad leg before reaching for the plant itself.

Rising, she scooted around him into the kitchen and placed it back inside the empty cardboard box on the counter. Hopefully she could save the pretty asparagus fern. "What are *you* doing here? I mean, this is your house, but your unit isn't scheduled to return until June—ohmigod."

Suddenly the dizziness returned. The only possible reason for Adam being here… The same reason he'd come back to Destiny a year ago.

Two months ago.

She spun around and grabbed for the granite countertop to keep upright. "Are you here as an official escort again? Please tell me you aren't responsible for another—"

Fay cut off her outburst, capturing her bottom lip with her teeth, but it was too late. As soon as the unfinished sentence left her mouth, she wished she could take it back.

She'd hurled a similar awful accusation at him eight weeks ago. To go there again, to make them both relive her resentment and hurt, would be of no use to anyone.

Besides, she couldn't say for certain whom she was mad at anymore. Whom she blamed.

Adam's eyes widened in surprise, before a flicker of hurt passed over them. Then with a blink, the emotions vanished.

"Responsible for what, Fay?" His features hardened as he slowly walked toward her. "For another member of my unit getting killed?"

"I'm sorry. Please forgive me." Fay forced herself to look him in the eye. "That was wrong. I shouldn't have said that."

The stiffness in Adam's posture eased. "You showed up two months ago determined to say what was on your mind. I listened, but that doesn't mean I agreed with you. Your words were coming from a place of anger and grief. I understood that."

"I wasn't looking for your understanding." The pain flared to life again inside her. "I was looking for—"

"Someone to blame. Yeah, I figured that out...afterward."

After they'd made love.

He didn't say the words aloud, but Fay knew exactly what he meant.

"It's been a rough year," he continued, his voice softer, "for you and the Coggens. You lost your husband, they lost their only son. And I lost my best friend."

Fay thought back to the first couple of weeks after Scott's funeral. She'd just begun to crawl out of her haze. She had to. Bills had to be paid, her business required her attention and Scott's parents, devastated at the loss of their only child, needed care. Finally needed her.

Then the house of cards Scott had so carefully constructed over the years to hide his misuse of their personal finances started to collapse. The second mortgages on their house, credit cards she never knew he had.

Not to mention what he'd done to his family's business.

A wave of exhaustion washed over Fay. A sudden desire to lean against Adam's chest, to feel the strength of his arms, filled her. To have someone take care of her for once.

Instead, she moved past him and sank into a chair at the dining room table. "You have no idea what we— What I've been through."

"You're right. I don't." He turned and faced her. "But somewhere between blame and the next morning, we found— Dammit, I don't know what we found."

She could feel him staring at her. *Don't ask me, please, don't ask.*

"Do you?"

She closed her eyes, and despite the silence, knew he'd walked to the table as a crisp clean scent that clung to his skin teased her nose. "Do I what?"

"Do you know what happened between us?"

Fay didn't have any idea how she was supposed to view those wonderful hours she's spent in Adam's arms. Guilt swamped her, and she swayed between remorse and pleasure remembering what they shared that night.

What they created that night.

How often she'd dreamed of that night happening again.

"It was an escape." Again, the words rushed past her lips before she could stop them. "A break from the real world, a moment we took…to block out our grief."

Stillness filled the air. She opened her eyes and found Adam's hands curled tight around the back of the chair he stood behind.

"Do you still blame me?" he asked.

Fay opened her mouth, but the words wouldn't come. Even now, she struggled to comprehend what Scott had done. Laying blame on her husband didn't do any good. The rationale she'd held on to for months was if Scott had never joined the service, he never would've been in Afghanistan, he wouldn't have died and…

And what?

Her life would've gone on as before? Is that what she really wanted?

Fay didn't know, but it didn't matter. Being this close to Adam was so confusing. Blaming him had been the constant she'd clung to as her world fell apart. Confronting him had seemed right. But since then, even before she found out she was carrying his child, the lines between right and wrong, blame and acceptance, had blurred.

She needed to get out of here.

"Fine, whatever. I guess we both should move forward." He released the chair and stepped away. "So, to totally switch gears, you never did tell me what you're doing in my house and how you got my security code."

"I'm here to clean."

His eyes widened. He was surprised. As surprised as she'd been when she'd answered the phone that morning at her shop to find out why Elise Murphy had called. "Your mother hired me to spruce up your place, from the cobwebs in the rafters downward, before your homecoming. Next week."

"My mother's been dragging my dad on a tour of the western half of the U.S. for the past two months."

"Yes, and because she wasn't here to do it herself, she asked me." Fay stood, dug the set of keys from her pocket and laid them on the table. "She gave me the code and told me to get the keys from Laurie, which I did. Good thing for you I'm just about done, except for that mess."

He reached for her when she started to turn, taking her arm. His hand, big and strong, yet gentle in its hold, slowly slid downward.

It was the first time he'd touched her since…

His thumb swept across the inside of her wrist, and she wondered if he could feel the pounding in her pulse. She raised her gaze to his.

His eyes darkened. "You've really been coming here and cleaning?"

"Considering the condition you left this place in, it was needed." She pulled from his grasp. "You're lucky you have such great parents."

"I didn't have time to clean up before I left. Remember?"

Oh, she remembered.

Walking in that first day had taken her breath away. Seeing the blankets still on the floor caused the memories of their lovemaking to rush back to her.

Waking in his arms, the emotional onslaught of shame over what they'd done and the unrelenting truth of how much she wanted him again. Grabbing her clothes. Racing to the bathroom to get dressed. Adam stepping out of his bedroom in his camouflage battle dress uniform.

The regret she could read on his face.

She'd tried to put the memories out of her mind as she worked, reminding herself she was getting paid for this job. More than that, she was doing a favor for Alastair and Elise Murphy. Adam's parents had been so nice to her over the last six months. There'd been no way she could've said no.

"Well, I guess your mom's idea worked for both of us." Fay crossed the kitchen and pulled out a broom and dustpan from the pantry. "You've got a sparkling home, and I got some much-needed cash."

"My mom is paying you?"

Fay didn't look at him as she bent to sweep up the remains of the pot. "What's wrong with that?"

"What about your shop? Are you still open for business?"

Six days a week. The pregnancy was making her more tired than she'd ever been in her life, but taking it easy wasn't something she could afford at the moment. "My shop is just fine, but a little extra money never hurts."

He crossed his arms over his chest. "Are you strapped for cash?"

"No." Surprised at how easy the second lie she'd told today fell from her lips, she dumped the broken pieces into the trash. "This was just a side job, and now that you're home, there's no need for me to come back."

"Fay—"

"I need to go." Her control over her wayward emotions faded fast. She had to get out of here before she burst into tears. Or worse. Walking past him, she gave him a wide berth, pausing to grab her purse and keys from the table. "I have to get back to the shop."

"No one knows I'm home yet."

She paused, her hand on the handle, not turning around.

"I arrived yesterday, ahead of everyone else," Adam

continued, his voice carrying across the room, "but just so you know, the return date for the entire unit has been moved up. You should be getting notified."

Tears burned at the back of her eyes. Why would she be called about the new date? It wasn't like she had anyone coming home.

"I'm trying to lay low," Adam went on, "get used to being home before I see…anyone."

"Don't worry." A sob caused her breath to hitch as she yanked open the door. "Your secret is safe with me."

Adam waited until late Saturday afternoon before heading to the Murphy family compound. There was no sign of his parents' RV camper even though they'd emailed everyone this morning to say they'd be home by dinnertime.

He pulled his pickup truck into the parking area at the rear of the sprawling two-story log home that also served as the corporate office for Murphy Mountain Log Homes, and cut the engine.

He sat for a moment and took in the buildings and grounds. A feeling of peace filled him.

The first person he saw was his niece, Abby.

Nolan's oldest child, she sat in the gazebo that was a thirtieth-anniversary gift from him and his brothers to their parents a decade ago. Head bent, her long blond hair hid her face as she concentrated on whatever she held in her hands.

He got out of his truck and headed up the path toward her. The sun was warm through the cotton material of his short-sleeved shirt. Boy, it felt good to be in civilian clothes again, to be wearing cowboy boots instead of combat boots.

Abby evidently didn't hear him approach. As soon as he saw her fingers flying over the smooth keyboard of her cell phone he knew why. So he leaned against the open door frame. "Hey, is this the Murphy place?"

Her head shot up. "Yeah?"

He tugged down his mirrored sunglasses and peeked at her over the rim. A wide smile came over her face.

"Uncle Adam!"

Jumping into his arms, she gave him a big hug. Abby and her brothers were visiting their mother in Boston when he was last home in April, so it'd been eleven months since he'd seen them. What a difference a year made.

"Boy, have you gotten tall." He returned her hug, set her down and righted his sunglasses. "And even prettier, if that's possible. Where are the twins?"

Abby grinned at his compliment and rolled her eyes. "You mean Tweedledum and Tweedledumber? Probably inside playing video games on Uncle Dev's computer."

Adam laughed. "Is that any way to talk about your brothers?"

"I've heard you all calling each other worse names than that," she shot back. "Most of which I'm not allowed to repeat."

"Hey, those weren't meant for young ears."

She tucked her phone into her pocket. "My ears turned sixteen last winter."

"Something I'm sure your father is thrilled about." Adam laid an arm across her shoulders. "Where is everyone?"

She gestured toward the main house. "Having their usual Saturday afternoon wrap-up before a family barbeque. Nana and Pop are coming home today. Aren't you supposed to be overseas?"

"Yep, so let's surprise them." Adam headed up the walkway, his niece tucked in close next to him. "Glad school is out?"

He listened as Abby chattered about her summer plans, his gaze moving around the family's property that bordered a lake with an official Indian name too difficult to pronounce so everyone just called it "the lake." There were two smaller log homes that sat nestled in the surrounding trees and the skeletal framing of a third that stood closer to the water near the boathouse.

Nolan had moved into the larger home with his three kids after they'd moved back to Destiny a couple of years ago. According to an email from his mother, the newlyweds, Bryant and Laurie, occupied the one-bedroom cabin where he'd lived for a few years. What he couldn't see was the log chapel situated deeper in the woods his family had built and where Bryant and Laurie were married last fall.

They entered the main house through his mother's kitchen, right off the oversize deck. The large and sunny room, like the rest of the place, had grown and changed over the years as the family and the business had. Back here, and the two wings on either side, was where his three single brothers still lived along with his folks.

The front of the house was comprised of offices, conference rooms, a wide staircase that led to the second-story guest quarters and a reception area that doubled as a gathering spot for clients, staff and, on the weekends, family.

A hard kick of anticipation landed in Adam's stomach. This past year had been tough, especially with his unit losing two of its own during this last tour. Escorting the body of his best friend home the previous summer had been the hardest duty Adam had ever done during his twenty years of service.

Despite all that, he was damn glad to be back in Destiny.

"Dad said you wouldn't be back for another week." Abby looked up at him and grinned. "Wait here. I'll let him know someone wants to see him. They're all gonna be stupefied when you walk into the room."

His niece's unique description was a step above the reaction he'd gotten yesterday from Fay.

Waiting out of sight on the other side of the large log archway, his mind went back to everything he and Fay had said—and didn't say—to each other.

Much like he'd done ever since she'd walked out his door.

He wanted to call her, to see if she was feeling all right. She'd looked so tired. But every time he grabbed his cell phone, something kept him from dialing her number.

His plan to steer clear was going to be impossible to keep. He'd known that the moment he'd first seen her, touched her.

Except he was sure Fay didn't feel the same way.

"Hey, Dad, you got a visitor outside." Abby's voice carried across the room. "Can I show him in?"

"Now?" His brother's reply was laced with irritation.

Adam grinned. Nolan was the next in line after him, younger with less than two years separating them, so his annoyance was nothing new.

"The last thing I want right now is to put on a happy face for a client."

"How about for a brother?" Adam stepped out and headed for the U-shaped seating area in front of the large stone fireplace. "Can *I* put a grin on that ugly mug of yours?"

Chaos broke out as everyone jumped to their feet and rushed him. Nolan reached him first, his smile broad and sincere. Adam found himself returning hugs with each of his brothers and high-fiving his thirteen-year-old nephews who came to see what all the noise was about.

He ignored Dev's whispered comment about owing him for keeping his mouth shut, congratulated his kid brother Ric on earning his college degree and ended with giving his new sister-in-law a big kiss since he'd missed seeing her in April, as she'd been traveling on company business.

"Well done, you two." He shot Bryant a wink. "Glad that brother of mine finally made an honest woman of you."

"When I told him he either had to marry me or find himself a new senior management accountant, he finally came around." Laurie grinned. "We're sorry you couldn't be there for the ceremony."

"No worries." He'd had a trip home planned last October for the wedding, but his plans had been changed at the last minute, courtesy of the U.S. military. "Glad you went ahead without me. We Murphy boys aren't just good-looking. We're smart, too."

"Smart enough to stay single," Liam called out, returning from the kitchen with handfuls of cold beers. "At least some of us are. Here, bro. You must be wanting one of these."

Before he could take a sip from the bottle, Adam spotted his parents as they entered the main room through the archway he'd used moments ago. It gave him a thrill to see both of them looking tanned, fit and happy.

"Well, this is a fine welcoming committee." The clear, sweet voice of Elise Murphy rose over their chatter as she walked into the room. "I expected to find everyone out enjoying this beautiful day and someone manning the grill already..."

Adam stepped out from behind his brothers, who all stood at close to six feet, to face his parents, smiling when his mother stopped short, her words fading when she spotted him. "Sorry, Mom. I guess we got a little carried away talking."

"Adam!" Elise Murphy raced to him and he pulled her into his arms, easily lifting the petite woman off her feet. "Oh, you're home!"

Chapter Three

The noise level in the room rose again as the entire Murphy clan joined in welcoming their parents home, but Adam became lost in his mother's reverent whispered prayers of thanks and the warm dampness of her tears against his neck.

"I can't believe you're finally here," she said, cradling his face in her hands when Adam set her feet back on the floor. "And early, too!"

"Home for good, Mom." Adam pressed a kiss to her forehead as she released him.

Switching his beer from one had to the other, he kept one arm around her shoulders while returning his father's strong handshake. But he was momentarily confused by the look in the older man's eyes.

It reminded him of when he was a kid. Like all parents, his dad had an uncanny ability of finding out when one of his children had done something wrong before the offender got the chance to confess.

In the past forty-eight hours? Without leaving his house?

Adam didn't think so.

"It's good to have you home, son." Alistair Murphy pulled him into a quick hug, complete with the familiar hearty slap to the back. "Real good."

"Thanks, Dad."

Adam took a long pull on his beer as everyone sat except the teenagers, who disappeared again with a warning to come back when the dinner preparations started. He then explained how he was able to return to the States ahead of his unit, admitting he spent the last two days holed up alone at his place.

Not exactly the truth, but there was no reason to go into Fay's visit.

The gleam in Dev's eye told him his brother was about to mention the mystery of his clean house. Adam quickly turned the conversation to Liam and Bryant, who gave details on the day-to-day running of the business. Then Dev weighed in on the company's home security program and Nolan spoke about their latest design projects with customers from Hollywood's A-list to Washington, D.C.'s power players.

Impressed, Adam felt even surer of his plans to concentrate on his ranch, knowing his younger brothers were handling things just fine without him. Although retired, their father was still involved in the company, as evidenced by the way he jumped into the conversation here and there. He even solicited Adam's opinion a few times, but Adam didn't take the bait, seeing no reason for his father to expect him to come back to the fold.

"Okay, enough business talk. Let's get this barbeque going. I'm ready for a steak, blood-rare," Alistair Murphy commanded, and soon everyone fell in, heading to the kitchen or the back deck to do their assigned chore.

Except Adam, who found himself alone with his parents, who asked him what his plans were now. Not ready to discuss his ideas yet, he told them the next few weeks were for nothing but getting reaccustomed to civilian life.

"I haven't had a vacation in years," he said with a smile. "I think I've earned some time off."

"Of course you have, dear." His mother patted his arm. "This is why I'm so glad Fay agreed to get your place spiffed up for you. Did she get everything done in time?"

Fay had done much more than just clean up the mess he'd left behind, something he'd only noticed after she'd walked out yesterday. "Yeah, the house looks great. I was really surprised."

"Good, that was the idea." Elise rose from the sofa. "Now, we better get dinner on the table or it'll be dark before I can start emptying that camper."

"Can I ask you something first?" Pushing to his feet, Adam addressed both his parents. "Scott's been gone almost a year now. How is Fay doing? How are his folks?"

His father stood and his parents glanced at each other before looking back at him. Why did he have a feeling he wasn't going to like what they had to say?

"We told you about Scott's father suffering a stroke just after New Year's," his father said.

"Yeah, I visited Walter and Mavis at the nursing home back in April." Adam crossed his arms over his chest. "The staff said his condition requires round-the-clock care."

Elise nodded. "Mavis sold their home in town and moved to a small apartment in Cheyenne near the facility. She goes every day to see him. She sits for hours and reads or talks to him. Losing their only child...I can't even begin to imagine their heartbreak."

"With Scott's death and Walter unable to be involved with Coggen Motors any longer, Walter's partner took over the entire business. All six dealerships," his father added.

"You mean he bought out the Coggens' and Fay's shares?" Adam asked.

Again with the shared looks between his parents.

"Honey, you know what a thriving gossip chain Destiny has." His mother finally spoke. "There have been rumors that Fay's been dealing with—"

"Well, look who's here!" Alastair Murphy's booming voice cut off whatever his wife was about to say. "Welcome, Fay."

Adam turned.

Fay stood in the entry area near the receptionist desk, balancing two flower arrangements in her arms and a surprised expression on her face. She looked very different from yesterday. Today she wore a dress, sweater and heels, all in matching shades of pink, with her curly hair lying in soft waves to her shoulders.

"Ah, hello." Her gaze darted between Adam and

his parents until she focused on him again. "The front doors were unlocked, so I came in thinking Bryant or Liam might still be… Well, I didn't expect any of you to be here."

Adam started toward her, registering the same exhaustion on her face, but his mother hurried past him and reached Fay first.

"My, aren't these pretty? They're the silk arrangements we talked about for the upstairs rooms, right?" She took one of the flower-filled vases out of Fay's arms, cradled it in her own and gave Fay a quick hug. "Oh, Al and I got back from our adventures just a little while ago. Everyone is out back fixing dinner for us. And for Adam! As you can see, Adam's home!"

Fay gave his mother a gentle smile. The simple act transformed her features, as if someone had finally turned a light on inside of her. The unexpected change caused Adam to stop midstride.

It was the first time in years he'd seen a real smile from her. Not since Scott had shocked her—and Adam—by following in his footsteps to join the Air Force six years ago.

His friend had come to him to talk about his plans, after another night of drinking at the Blue Creek, but Adam had been too caught up in his own hell at the time with Julia to do anything but get his buddy home in one piece. By the time he'd finally surfaced from the mess of his divorce, Scott had completed boot camp and had been assigned to his reserve unit.

After that, his friendship with Fay cooled. When Scott had received orders for a tour overseas it had disappeared entirely.

"Yes, I do see that," Fay replied to his mother, then she turned to look at him. "Welcome home, Adam."

Her smile looked forced now. But Adam decided he would take what he could get even when she turned her attention to his father.

"Al, it's nice to have you and Elise back in Destiny, too."

"It's good to be home," his father said. "You'll stay for dinner?"

Fay shook her head. "No, thank you. I just wanted to drop these off before I headed back to my shop. I'd planned to come by this morning on my way to Ch- Cheyenne, but I was running late."

Did she go down to Cheyenne to visit with her former in-laws? Is that why she looked like she'd been put through a wringer?

"You sure you can't stay?" Adam asked, wanting the chance to spend more time with her. "We'd love to have you with us."

She looked at him for a long moment, an unreadable emotion in her eyes. "No, I can't stay."

Her words had an edge to them Adam couldn't un- derstand. She seemed almost angry. Because of their re- union yesterday? That hadn't gone the way he wanted, but Fay had charged out of his place so fast, he'd barely had time to gather his thoughts.

"Oh, I think these beautiful blooms are going to match with the quilt in the suite upstairs perfectly!" Elise chimed in, breaking the silence. "I'm going to head up and see for myself. Be back in a jiffy!"

Adam grinned, watching his mother dash away. Some people walked, but Elise had always moved at a speed that spoke of a mother who raised six boys. "She's been keeping you busy, hasn't she?"

"Fay's actually helping out with the model homes," Al said. "We contracted her about six months ago to provide arrangements for the homes, guest quarters and the office. She now oversees the exterior landscaping as well."

This was news to Adam. Even though he wasn't involved in the day-to-day running of the business, he was surprised no one in the family mentioned it in their letters. "I guess that means you're the one responsible for my new front yard as well?"

"I just added a few bushes and flowers to enhance the trees and lawn." Fay looked down, her attention on the silk flowers in her arms. "Otherwise, it was just cleaning and straightening up."

"And new curtains, dishes and bedding." Adam rattled off the list of changes that had finally registered when he took the time to really see all the work Fay had done. "Sort of a mini *Extreme Makeover.*"

Her gaze shot back to his, uncertainty in her hazel eyes. "I kept asking your mother in our emails if she included you in any of the decorating changes. I'm sorry if there's something you don't like."

"I like it, Fay, all of it. You went above and beyond by getting my father to part with his treasured oil painting."

Adam had been stunned to find the original artwork depicting wild horses racing across an open field, the work of his great-grandfather, the first Alistair Murphy, hanging over his desk in the third bedroom.

"I've been after him for years to part with that painting. Believe me, I like everything you did to my home."

The doubt in her eyes gave way to a sparkle of delight. A rush of male pride filled his chest that his words were the reason why.

"Nolan and Liam came over and hung it themselves." Fay smiled as she nodded in his father's direction. "They said your dad insisted it belonged in the home of a rancher."

Adam's chest swelled at that bit of news, knowing the gesture represented more than just the handing down of a family heirloom.

Alistair Murphy cleared his throat. "Yes, well, I'm sure your brothers are fighting over control of the spatula by now. Time for me to play referee." He gave his son a genial pat on the shoulder before he walked away. "Son, do your best to change the lady's mind, okay?"

Adam waited until his dad left before deciding to take his advice. Suddenly he wanted nothing more than to share his homecoming celebration with her as well as his family. "So, what can I do to get you to stay?"

"N-nothing. I need—" Her smile faded and she brushed past him, heading for the stairs. "I'm going to take this other arrangement up to your mother and then go home."

"Fay." He followed, catching her as she started up the steps. "Please, wait. I want to talk to you."

She paused on the third riser. "It's been a long day, I missed lunch and talking is the last thing—"

"Okay, don't talk, just listen."

Shaking her head, she put one foot on the next step.

"I'm sorry." He followed, suddenly determined to

say what he should've said before she walked out of his house. "About yesterday. I never should've pushed you about your business or money or…or about what happened between us."

She whirled around, gripping the handrail with one hand. "Shh! Someone might hear—" Her voice broke and she closed her eyes. "Someone might…"

The sudden paleness of her features and the slight sway of her body sent off alarms inside him. Adam skipped two steps to get to her. "Fay, what is it? What's wrong?"

Her eyes fluttered a few times as she struggled to open them before she went boneless in his arms.

"Oh, my!" Elise called out. "Fay!"

His mother's voice carried over the inner balcony that circled the second floor and looked down on the great room, but Adam's focus remained on the unconscious woman in his arms. He grabbed the vase of flowers now wedged between their bodies and set it aside.

"Fay?" Cradling her shoulders with one arm, he gently tapped her soft cheek with his fingers. Her normally fair skin was a deeper shade of pale. "Honey, wake up."

When she didn't respond, he pushed away the panic that flared in his gut and easily hefted her into his arms. Turning, he continued up the stairs as Nolan and his dad returned to the room.

"What's going on?" Nolan asked.

"Fay passed out," Adam offered, but didn't stop as he heard his brother and father start up the stairs behind him.

He headed to the open door to the guest room his

mother was pointing to. Making sure not to catch Fay's heels on the doorway, he walked into the room and laid her gently on the queen-size bed.

Fay's eyelids fluttered open and he started to breathe again.

"What...what happened?"

Her soft whisper cut through his concern. "It's okay. You fainted right in the middle of talking to me."

Panic filled her beautiful eyes. "Fainted?"

"Don't worry, sweetie." Elise stepped in front of Adam and laid a hand on Fay's arm. "Adam caught you as soon as your knees buckled."

"I—I don't understand." Fay's soft voice grabbed at his heart. "I don't remember."

"It's all right, dear. You just take a few moments to lie here and relax. We know you've been battling the flu for a while now...." Adam's mother looked back at him over her shoulder. "Why don't you go downstairs and get Fay a glass of cool water?"

Leaving was the last thing he wanted to do, but he read the unspoken demand to get out in his mother's eyes. Adam did what he was told, closing the door behind him, only to meet his brother and dad just outside the door.

"Is she okay?" Alistair asked.

"What the hell happened?" Nolan demanded.

"I don't know." Adam answered both questions at the same time. "One minute we were talking and the next her eyes closed and she dropped."

The two men opposite him shared a look. If one more family member shared a look with another he'd hit something. Or someone. He'd rather someone start talking. Pronto.

"I'm going to put together a tray with a light lunch for Fay. She didn't get a chance to eat while she was visiting Walter and Mavis," Elise said, joining them as she too closed the door behind her. "You three leave that girl alone and let her rest."

"What's going on?" Adam asked. "You mentioned the flu. Is Fay sick?"

His mother continued on her way while his brother and father remained silent. Determined to find out how she was doing, Adam reached for the door, but his father's hand on his shoulder stopped him.

"Son, wait."

Adam turned back. "Wait for what?"

"I don't think you should go charging in there before we've had a chance to talk."

"About what?"

"There's something you should—" Nolan paused, then lowered his voice. "Over the last month or so I've noticed Fay hasn't been feeling well. She says it's a cold she can't shake, but when I mentioned it to Dad during our weekly phone calls he said the craziest thing I've ever heard. Then again, seeing the two of you together—"

"You only saw me carry her up the stairs. What the hell are you talking about?"

His father motioned Adam to follow him away from the door and down the hall. As much as he didn't want to, he went, his brother at his side.

"Son, during your last visit home in April I headed for your place early, wanting to spend some one-on-one time with you before we took you to the airport. Then I saw Fay's van in your driveway and hightailed it back home."

Every muscle in Adam's body stilled, even his heart for a moment. Then it began to slam inside his chest.

"You've always had a thing for her," Nolan added.

Adam's gaze shot to his brother, who only shrugged and continued. "Hey, I remember you telling me what happened between you two. Down by the river? The night of your twenty-first birthday?"

"Geez, that was years ago," Adam said. "We were just kids."

"Besides, between Dad and me we've been through this nine times—"

"Through what?"

"If we didn't know any better, your brother and I would both swear Fay is pregnant." His father once again placed a hand on his shoulder. "What happened that night? Is it possible you're the father?"

Pregnant?

His father's soft words exploded inside Adam's head. He braced himself, his posture ramrod straight against his father's touch, but the detonation continued, a powerful roar that flowed outward until it reached every inch of his body.

He'd felt this way only twice before in his life, most recently just a few short weeks ago when he'd had the harrowing experience of barely missing an IED— or improvised explosive device—that thankfully exploded after their transport of construction equipment had passed and was a few precious miles away.

Adam tried to form the word he hadn't spoken in

five long years, but he couldn't put the syllables together aloud. That didn't stop the utterance from vibrating inside his head again.

Pregnant?

Because of the night they spent together?

He'd insisted they use protection, both times, even after Fay had whispered something about it not being necessary as she couldn't get...

Fay being sick yesterday morning at his place. The way she held one hand protectively over her stomach. The paleness of her skin, the tiredness in her eyes.

The way she pulled from his touch.

"I know this is the last thing you expected to return home to, but if this does turn out to be true, I know you, son. You won't turn away—" Alistair stopped when Laurie appeared at the top of the stairs balancing a food-laden tray in her hands.

"Elise asked me to bring this up to Fay," she said, then looked directly at her brother-in-law. "By the way, the twins took washing up for dinner to a new level. Complete with soapy water and squirt guns."

Nolan groaned and headed for the stairs. "I better get down there."

"That looks heavy," Adam spoke before he even realized what he said. "Here, let me take it into her."

She released the tray to him, a quizzical look on her face. "Are you sure? Elise said something about Fay being a bit light-headed and embarrassed—"

"I'm sure." He forced a grin and managed to keep it there when his gaze locked with his father's. "Don't worry. I'll be... It'll be okay."

His father nodded and Adam turned and headed for the guest room.

It'll be okay?

He had a feeling nothing was going to be okay ever again if his father and brother's suspicions were correct.

He knocked once and waited a moment, then entered. The first thing he noticed was that Fay had removed her shoes. One of his mother's handmade quilts covered her, but her bare feet peeked out from the bottom edge of the patchworked material. Her toes were painted vivid neon pink.

His gaze slowly traveled up the length of her, taking in the curves hidden beneath the blanket, pausing at where her hands rested against her stomach.

His gut clenched, but he continued his gaze upward. Until he reached her face and found her staring back at him, her cheeks matching the bright shade on her feet.

She scooted up higher against the pillows until she sat upright in the middle of the bed. "Adam! I wasn't—I thought your mother—"

"She's busy playing grandma to Nolan's hellions..." His voice trailed off as he realized the woman in front of him may very well be carrying another Murphy grandchild.

His child.

Forcing himself to move forward, Adam walked to the side of the bed and waited.

Fay's eyes remained focused on the tray.

"You said you skipped lunch," he finally said. "That's probably why you—"

"Yes, the availability of food where Walter is isn't

the best and Mavis didn't want me to… Well, it's been a long…a long day."

He set the tray on her lap, the contents of the glass of milk sloshing over the rim. He tightened his grip just as Fay's hands flew up to steady the tray. Their hands collided, her touch cool as her fingers circled his wrists.

Remaining perfectly still, Adam focused on the viselike grip Fay had on him. Knuckles whitening, she sucked in a deep breath, a shudder layered with a hiss and then a whispered sob.

He looked at her then, watching her bite hard on her bottom lip as twin tears leaked from beneath her closed eyelids.

"Fay, please." His voice held a deep rasp. "Don't cry. Not over spilled milk."

Another sob, this time combined with a light chuckle. "I—I can't help it. Lately, the craziest things… A sappy commercial, a country love song on the radio, the sight of a woman holding—"

She cut off her words, but Adam knew what she was going to say. "A woman holding a baby?"

She jerked her head in a quick nod.

The action caused him to sink to the bed, his hip pressed against the wooden legs of the tray, the strength in his legs suddenly gone.

She released her hold on him then, her fingers quickly brushing across her moist cheeks. "I'm sorry. Please, just ignore me—"

"Fay, are you pregnant?"

Her hands stilled.

She finally opened her eyes and looked at him, fresh tears already replacing those she'd erased.

"Yes."

"The baby's mine?" He'd already known what her answer would be, the truth embedded deep in his heart as unquestioning as his love for his family, his land and his country. But he asked anyway.

Her shoulders drew back, and she lifted her chin a notch in a proud motion. Dropping her hands, she returned his stare. "This baby is mine."

"That's where you're wrong." His reply was swift, sure and absolute. "This baby is ours."

Chapter Four

The strength and conviction in Adam's statement both soothed and terrified her.

Stark fear had enveloped her when she'd awakened in his arms and learned she'd fainted in the middle of their discussion on the stairs. As soon as his mother had ushered him from the room, Fay knew she had to get out of there, no matter how much her stomach welcomed the thought of the promised lunch.

But then Adam had returned.

The way he'd looked at her, his eyes warm yet filled with questions. The act of setting a tray of food down in front of her, the light teasing over spilled milk.

Simple things that released those blasted hormones raging inside her and brought forth the never-ending supply of tears.

How had he known to even ask her such a question? And shouldn't she at least be a little upset that he'd somehow guessed her secret instead of feeling the rush of relief that filled her now that he knew about the baby?

"Fay?"

The low timbre of Adam's voice made her blink. She realized she'd been staring at the simple yet colorful garden salad and buttered roll that accompanied the glass of milk on the tray.

She was hungry.

"Fay, we need to talk."

She reached for the fork. "I need to eat."

Adam rose from the bed without disturbing the food. With her mouth full she couldn't ask if he was leaving.

He wasn't. Dragging an armless chair that looked too delicate to support his six-foot-plus frame closer to the bed, he sat again, arms folded across his chest as he watched her take another bite.

She should be thinking of escaping, but her body's need for nutrition seemed to have overridden everything else. The creamy dressing on the salad was hitting all the right taste buds.

Yummy.

Fay instinctively knew she'd be able to keep this meal down. Thank goodness. Ever since finding out Adam was back in town yesterday morning she hadn't been able to eat anything except crackers.

Then again today being the one Saturday a month she visited with Walter and Mavis meant she'd been feeling queasy all day anyway.

She hated going to that nursing home. Hated the way Mavis slipped further and further into the past, retelling stories from years ago of their happy little family.

The years before their son had the nerve to marry beneath him.

Before their son had destroyed all their lives.

Pushing aside the memories, Fay concentrated on her food. Eating slowly, she savored every bite, even though she felt like a science experiment on display, pinned by the intensity of Adam's gaze.

"You're staring."

"I know."

She finished off the roll, followed by a long sip of milk. Oh, that was good. "Stop it."

"You're looking better already."

Hmm, how should she take that remark? "Better than what?"

One side of his mouth rose in a half grin. A light flutter crossed Fay's insides that she quickly blamed on finally having a full stomach. "Deathly pale isn't a good color for you."

She stilled, her hands falling to her lap.

"Ah, damn, I didn't mean—"

Adam dropped his arms and leaned forward. Bracing his elbows on his knees, he looked like he was going to reach for her hand, but then laced his fingers together instead. "I'm sorry. That was a stupid thing to say."

"It's okay." Fay waved off his apology. She'd always been a little too much like Casper the Friendly Ghost when it came to her skin tone. "I know you didn't— I know what you meant."

"How long have you known..." He paused and swallowed, his gaze steady, but with a hint of uncertainty. "About the pregnancy?"

Her fingers shook as she reached for the chilled dish

of fresh strawberries. Grabbing a small one, she held it to her lips, debating if she should use the tasty-looking dessert as a stalling technique.

She wasn't ready for this conversation, but like so many other events that had happened over the past year, she needed to once again step up and face things, face Adam, head-on.

Besides, the man deserved an answer.

"Almost a week now."

Surprise filled his eyes. "That's all?"

She took a bite, the juice a little sweet, a little tart on her tongue. "I've been fighting a cold off and on since February," she answered after a quick swallow. "I thought I'd finally got over it back in April, but then the tiredness and upset stomach started again a few weeks ago."

"But you're okay?" His gaze quickly traveled the length of her, and Fay's body heated beneath the light-weight quilt. "You're both okay?"

He was the first one to ask about the health of her baby—their baby—and the waterworks threatened again. She blinked hard and nodded, reaching for another berry, pausing to dip it in the remains of the salad dressing before she took a bite.

Hmm, not bad. She repeated the action just to be sure. Yep, that tasted pretty good.

"You do realize that's ranch dressing you're using?"

Fay nodded and found herself smiling at the baffled expression on Adam's face. "I'd prefer whipped cream, but this works, too."

His dark brown eyes heated for a moment, then it was gone. No, that couldn't be right. Except for that crazy night they'd spent together two months ago, Adam had never looked at her that way.

That wasn't exactly true.

Fay concentrated on eating another ranch-dipped berry, her mind racing with the memory of another time, years ago.

She'd been out riding her bike when she'd found him celebrating his birthday down near the bend of the Blue Creek River, a favorite spot over the years of the high school crowd for swimming and parties. That night it'd been just him, a six-pack and the Murphy family dog, whose name she couldn't remember.

What she did remember was how they'd talked.

About their unknown futures, how far away high school seemed now that they were both in college, laughing over the day they'd met. She'd been pleasantly surprised when Adam revealed how he wished he'd asked her out on a date before his best friend had.

Then she'd shared the packaged cupcakes she'd kept hidden in her purse, sang him an off-key version of "Happy Birthday" and impulsively leaned over to give him a kiss on the cheek.

A kiss that missed when he turned his head.

Their lips collided. And stayed. The kiss deepened, his arms encircling her, her going willingly when he gently laid her down in the sweet summer grass.

Minutes later, a group of kids raced by, hollering out car windows, and they'd sprung apart. Adam blamed the beer, Fay blamed herself. Both swore it was no big deal and promised never to mention it again.

Her face heated for the second time today.

Not only at the memory of the secret pleasure and

embarrassment she'd felt all those years ago, but for how much she enjoyed being in his company right now.

How could that be? After the anger and blame she'd carried deep inside all these months?

"Fay? Are you all right?" Adam leaned in closer. "You look a little flushed."

"I'm fine." The berries were gone. She'd finished them off while lost in the past. Placing the bowl back on the tray, she moved it, and the quilt, off her lap. "I really need to get going."

He straightened. "I think we still have a few things to discuss."

"Can't we do this later?" She swung her legs off the bed and slipped on her shoes. "Your family must be holding dinner for you."

He stood when she did. Fay would've taken a step away, but the bed pressed against the back of her knees. Even though she was in heels, he towered over her. Her gaze locked on the tanned skin displayed by the open collar of his shirt.

Oh, the tingling sensations from yesterday were back. It was definitely time to leave. "Peggy's been alone all day at the shop. I have to get back to close up."

"Who's Peggy?"

"My part-time help, Peggy Katz." She sidestepped away from him and reached for her purse on a nearby dresser. "She's been working for me since last fall."

"Ah, the pretty blonde with the great smile?"

She paused in her search for her keys, ignoring the flare of…of whatever was inside her that hated how he perfectly described her employee. "Yes, that's her. I didn't know you knew each other."

"We don't. Devlin mentioned her a few times in his emails."

Ah, yes. His playboy brother had been hanging around the shop more and more recently. "She's newly divorced."

"Yeah, Dev mentioned that, too."

Of course he did. Fay shook her head. She was going to have to sit the young woman down for a friendly chat when it came to getting involved with the Murphy brothers.

Yeah, like you're one to talk.

But she wasn't involved with Adam Murphy.

No, just having his baby.

Fay blocked out her irritating inner voice that sounded a bit too much like her employee who, despite the ten years that separated them, seemed wise beyond her years. She headed for the door. "I really do need to get back to the shop."

"I'll go with you." He lifted the tray from the bed with one hand and smoothed the quilt back into place with the other. "I think my family will understand me leaving. Considering the circumstances."

He was probably right. The Murphys were a wonderful, close-knit, multigenerational group that tripped over each others' lives, and not just because of the family business. The brothers were known to fight as hard as they played, but there was never any question of the love and support they had for each other—

Oh, no!

Someone in his family had figured out about the baby!

Guessed anyway, and told Adam as soon as he came

home. No, that couldn't be right. He would've said something as soon as they were alone.

She stepped out on the landing. "Who told you about...about me being pregnant?"

"My father."

"What?" Surprise flooded her veins. "Your parents have been gone for the past two months."

Adam shrugged as he took her arm and started walking toward the stairs. "Actually Nolan was the first to notice you being sick. They put two and two together during a few phone calls, although it was just suspicion. Until now."

"But how did they connect us?" She was grateful to see the room empty as they started down the stairs. Facing his family was the last thing she wanted. "I mean, no one would ever think that we would—"

"Does it really matter? I think the bigger question is when were *you* planning on telling me about the baby?"

An edge laced Adam's voice even as his touch remained gentle and supportive. Not that she needed his help. She was feeling much better and perfectly capable of walking down a flight of stairs.

Fay pulled from his grasp once they were on level ground again. "I was waiting for the right time."

"Yesterday morning when you came out of my bathroom would've been perfect."

He was right, but the shock of seeing him again, sooner than she expected, combined with her mortification at getting sick...it had all been too much.

"Adam—"

"How about when I asked why you were sick?" He

continued. "Or maybe when I tried to talk about what happened that night between us."

"Adam, I've only know about this for a little while. It's been a long day, a long couple of months, a long year. Not to put too light a spin on things, but I've had a lot to deal with and my day isn't over yet."

Tears threatened again, but Fay fought them off. She wanted to be—should be—angry with him. That's how she'd felt toward this man for a long time. But the feeling wouldn't come.

In fact, entirely different feelings were bombarding her from all directions and she didn't have time to deal with them either.

"Please stay with your family and let me deal with my shop. It's not like either of us is going anywhere. We'll talk. Soon. I promise."

He looked at her for a long moment with those amazing chocolate-brown eyes that spoke of truth and strength and always doing the right thing.

No, wait. That wasn't how she saw him.

Not anymore.

She'd lived for years with a burning resentment over the fact Adam had been the one who convinced Scott to join the military. A resentment that burned like fire after she got word of Scott's death.

How could spending less than an hour in his company take her back to the long-forgotten emotions she'd carried deep inside her when they were both so young?

"Okay, then I'll walk you out," he said, before setting the tray on a nearby chair.

No, she had to get away from him, the sooner the better. "That's not necessary."

"Maybe not, but I'm going to do it anyway." He waved toward the front door. "Let's go."

Accepting that arguing would only keep her in his company longer, Fay headed for the foyer. Adam fell into step next to her as they left the cool air-conditioning for the warm sunshine. They walked to the parking lot, and he waited while she climbed inside the flower shop van, the only vehicle she still owned.

Because he remained standing outside the van and it would've been rude not to, she rolled down the driver's-side window.

"You sure you're feeling well enough to drive?" he asked.

"I'm fine."

His features relaxed when she pulled on her seat belt. "Drive safe."

"I'm sure you're as stunned by this news as I was. We'll talk in a day or two." A quick twist of the key and the engine turned over. Thankfully. "I just need a little time to make some decisions."

Make some decisions.

Adam stood in the gravel parking lot, watching the woman pregnant with his child drive away. He stood there, even after that ratty old van of hers disappeared around the curve in the road. Fay's parting words echoed inside his head until they meshed with a long-ago, locked-away memory.

The words of another woman, about another baby.

It's my decision. It's my body. I never wanted this.

He and Julia had married too fast after dating too little, and before they'd even reached their two-year anniversary, he found a positive home pregnancy test in the trash. After managing to hold out three days, waiting for her to share the news, he'd finally asked. He was so overjoyed when she nodded yes, he'd mistaken her tears for happy ones.

Then her stunning pronouncement, his attempts at soothing her fears, calming her doubts, pleading that turned into anger as he finally understood the decision she'd already made without him.

A decision that was taken out of their hands less than a week later, and just like that, his marriage was over.

"So, were we right?"

Adam's heart seized and he spun, his hands reaching for the M16 assault rifle he no longer carried with him everywhere.

His brother's shocked expression stopped him.

Dropping his hands, Adam pulled in a shaky breath. "Sorry. That was…stupid. You just surprised me."

"Yeah, I figured that out pretty quick." Nolan shoved his hands into his pockets, his mouth drawn into a frown before he continued. "Mom and Dad sent me to see if you and Fay were joining us. Since you're standing out here alone I'm guessing she ate and split?"

Adam sighed, knowing his brother must've seen the tray in the living room. "Yeah, she had to get back to the shop."

"And?"

Answering his brother with a quick nod, Adam turned and headed back inside.

"She didn't stay very long. Don't you two have a few things to talk about?" Nolan asked as they walked past the offices and through the great room, stopping long enough for Adam to grab the lap tray of dirty dishes. "Adam?"

Ignoring his brother's question when he heard voices coming from the kitchen, Adam stopped. "You haven't said anything about Fay to anyone else, have you? Other than Dad?"

"No, but you know the folks, they share everything. I'm sure he told Mom what he told me. The question now is what are you going to do about it?"

"Right now? Nothing."

"Huh?"

Adam pulled in a deep breath, willing the tension in his shoulders and chest to ease, but that same dread he'd felt years ago stayed with him. "Yes, Fay and I need to talk, to make some decisions, but she had to get back to work."

"Are you going over to see her later tonight?"

"I don't know." He hadn't planned on it. Fay had asked for a couple of days, but waiting that long to talk to her, hell, just to see her again, was going to be impossible.

What if she did something rash before he got a chance to have his say? Could he hold out until morning? The shop was closed on Sundays. "Look, I'd appreciate it if you kept this to yourself. I really have no idea what we're going to do next or where we go from here."

"Sure, I can keep a secret, but news like this isn't going to stay quiet for long. Not in a town this small."

Adam nodded in agreement, remembering how his mother had started to mention something about Fay when it came to the town's infamous rumor mill.

"Is there something else going on with Fay?" he asked. "I mean, other than what I just found out."

Nolan started to speak but was stopped from answering by the appearance of his daughter.

"Dad! Luke and Logan farted in the pool. Again." Abby's face screwed up in a glower as if she could smell the offending odor from here. "How am I going to have friends over? I can't believe they're turning thirteen in a few months."

Wrapping an arm around his daughter, Nolan gave her a quick kiss on the forehead as the three of them entered the kitchen. "Come on, we'll tag team 'em."

"Like I'm getting in that water? No way!"

Nolan headed outside with his daughter, passing Elise as she entered carrying a plate heaping with a juicy steak. Its tangy, mouthwatering smell caused Adam's stomach to growl in appreciation.

She smiled and motioned for her son to set down the tray. "Let's trade. You eat and I'll take care of that."

Adam didn't need to be told twice. He sat at the center island, taking the plate and silverware out of his mother's hands.

"Do you want another beer to go with that?" she asked.

He shook his head. No, he needed to keep his mind clear. "How about iced tea or lemonade instead?"

"Coming right up."

"And how about some information?"

He cut into the steak and placed a large piece in his mouth, muffling the moan that threatened to escape as soon as the tender meat touched his tongue.

Damn, it'd been a long time since he's had a meal like this.

He chewed, swallowed and cut another piece. "You were about to share what the local gossips were saying about Fay before she showed up."

His mother glanced out the large sliding glass doors at the rest of the family before joining Adam at the counter. Placing the tall glass of lemonade in front of him, she leaned closer. "I'll share if you will. Am I going to be a grandmother again?"

Adam couldn't stop his grin.

His mother gave a little squeal of joy and pressed a quick kiss to his cheek. "Oh, that is so wonderful!"

"Even though we've sort of gone about it the wrong way?"

"There is never anything wrong about a new life coming into this world," Elise said, grabbing his hand and giving it a quick squeeze. "It's about time you and Fay found some happiness in your lives. Why not with each other?"

If only it were that easy.

Adam straightened and took a quick swallow to cool his dry throat. "There isn't anything between Fay and me."

"You mean besides a child," his mother pointed out. "You know, I remember the three of you always running around together back in high school and college. You, Scott and Fay. Even back then I could see—"

"That was a long time ago." Adam pushed the pasta salad around on his plate. "Things, and people, change."

"And not always for the better. If only half of what was being said about that girl was true, poor Fay has been through so much. Not to mention the Coggens. All thanks to Scott, rest his soul."

Dread filled Adam's gut, taking away any thought of food. "What exactly has been going on around here this past year?"

Chapter Five

Adam walked slowly in the peace and quiet of the early morning. The harmonious sound of voices raised in song drifted from the white clapboard church he'd just slipped out of as the first Sunday service of the day was ending.

Arriving late, he'd sat alone in the very last pew and allowed the calm words of the preacher and the familiar hymns from his childhood to flow over him.

And he prayed.

He prayed for those still fighting overseas, those who'd returned safely and for the loved ones of those never coming home, at least not the way they'd planned. Like Scott and Carl, the two members of his unit killed during this last tour.

His last tour.

Stetson in hand, Adam soon reached the Coggen family plot in the far corner of the neighboring cemetery. He kept walking until he stood before his best friend's grave.

He didn't know what to say or if he had the right to say anything at all. Was it true? Had his buddy really screwed up so badly before he'd shipped out that his family was still paying for those mistakes a year after his death?

Stunned by what his mother shared with him yesterday, and the stories his father had added as they'd walked along the lake at sunset, he could only shake his head.

Scott's family had always been high on the town's pecking order when it came to money. While his friend had balked at working for his father right after college, eventually Scott started as a manager at the Laramie location of Coggen Motors, one of six dealerships located all over Wyoming, and worked his way up.

Now the entire business belonged to someone else.

Scott and Fay had built a fancy home on the other side of town on land given to them by Scott's parents who'd lived right next door. Only Fay had sold the house back in January, not long after Walter's stroke.

Something didn't add up.

Fay should've received a one-time death gratuity when Scott was killed. Not that it was a lot of money, but it would've helped. Not to mention she should be getting a monthly payment for survivors of deceased veterans. And what about the group life insurance every serviceman had?

If things were as bad financially for her as it sounded, how was she going to handle adding a baby to the mix?

His baby.

Not that he planned on money being an issue for her. No, he fully intended on taking financial responsibility for his child.

The enormity of what exactly that would entail stuck hard in his gut. Like dive bombers fixated on the same target, so many emotions came at him from all sides.

Anger, pain, guilt, grief. All mixed with the joyful news of the baby.

A joy he wasn't sure he deserved.

"I'm going to take care of her," he vowed, standing in the hushed silence. "I have no idea how, but I promise you that much."

A shaft of sunlight broke through the trees, landing on the smooth granite marker. He'd blinked hard, slapped his hat on his head and headed for his pickup truck.

Pulling away as the church started to empty, Adam drove to the local bakery. Moments later he turned off Main Street and pulled to a stop in the parking lot behind The Sudz Bucket, a do-it-yourself laundry, Ursula's Updos, the local beauty parlor and Fay's Flower Shop.

And for the last six months Fay's home as well.

Adam honestly hadn't planned on stopping by her apartment this morning. Just like he hadn't planned to stop by the church or Scott's grave.

Then he'd spotted the display of doughnuts back at the bakery and remembered how he and Fay had shared a preference for the simple glazed ones. Before he could talk himself out of it, he'd grabbed a variety, just in case her taste had changed, and here he was.

He pried off the lid to his coffee and took a sip from the steaming cup before glancing at his watch. Almost nine-thirty. Too early to walk the double flights of outside stairs and knock on her door?

Fay had asked yesterday for time to think. Said she had decisions to make. He wanted—he needed—to know the most basic decision of all.

Did she want the baby?

He shook his head, tossing aside the stupid question.

She had claimed the child as hers when he'd asked about the pregnancy. Still…he had to be sure. For whatever reason, she and Scott never had children during their marriage.

Was that Scott's idea or hers? If it was hers, how did she feel about getting pregnant now?

How did she feel that he was the father of her child?

Stop driving yourself crazy and go knock on the door. He took another sip.

What was he waiting for? An engraved invitation?

Forget it, pal. The lady couldn't get away from you fast enough yesterday.

And yeah, that stung a bit, too.

The rumbling of his stomach had him flipping open the box of doughnuts on the seat next to him and grabbing one. Gone in four bites. He reached for another.

As he brought it to his lips, Adam got the strangest feeling he was being watched. Looking out the side window, he found himself under the scrutiny of a mutt sitting on his haunches in the empty parking space next to his truck.

Scruffy looking, the dog's matted fur was more gray than white except for the large circle of black that covered one side of his face from the ear, over one eye and down along his snout.

"Well, where did you come from?" He rolled down the window, the action and his words causing the dog's tail to thump wildly against the pavement. "What? You think you're going to get some of my breakfast?"

Damn if the dog didn't nod his head.

Adam's mouth rose into a grin for the first time that day as he tossed the pastry toward the mutt. It was gone in a flash. He reached for an old-fashioned plain doughnut instead of a glazed one this time and it disappeared as quickly as the first.

"Sorry, the rest are spoken for." Adam looked up in time to see movement behind the partially closed curtains hanging in the large picture window on the second floor.

He grabbed the doughnuts and his coffee and got out of the truck, pausing to put on his hat. "You better head home now."

The dog got up on all four paws and offered a full-bodied shake that started at his head and traveled to the other end, a move that revealed no collar or the jangle of tags.

Great, a stray. Or maybe his identification had gotten loose and fallen off. "Sorry, bud, either way, I've got enough on my plate as it is."

Adam headed across the parking lot, the dog close on his heels. His own fault, he never should've fed him. Maybe if he ignored the mutt, he'd go away.

Taking the stairs two at a time, he soon stood at Fay's entryway, eyeing the patriotic wreath dressed with red, white and blue flowers through the outer screen door.

He wasn't alone.

"Go on, get out of here." Adam kept his voice low as he nudged the dog's back end gently with the toe of his boot. "No wingman needed this time."

The creature just sat there looking at him before he cocked his head toward the door.

Go on and knock, the shiny brown eyes seemed to say.

"Don't rush me," he whispered. "This isn't easy, you know."

The dog responded with a couple of sharp barks and seconds later the door sprung open.

"What's going on—" Fay's sleepy eyes widened. "Adam?"

Her hands flew to her fresh-from-bed mussed curls, quickly gathering the long strands into a messy ponytail. The jerky movements, arms raised and elbows askew, caused the silky robe she wore to gape from her collarbone to her knees.

Just enough for Adam to catch a glimpse of smooth skin, the sweet outer swells of her breasts and lacy green panties.

Whoa, ten-hut and standing tall.

A light breeze crossed the back of his neck and shoulders. Seconds later, the cool air touched her skin.

Everywhere.

Fay looked down, gasped and gathered the edges of her robe in her fists.

Adam felt the imaginary slap to the back of his head as sure as if his mother had been standing right there.

Forcing his gaze from Fay, he looked instead at the

dog who returned his stare. He could've sworn one bushy eyebrow rose in a mocking salute.

"You're actually taking credit for that?" he mumbled. "Okay, maybe you're good for something after all."

A quick glance back found Fay straightening her robe, knotting it tightly at her waist. He bit back a groan as she smoothed her hands down over her curves, pressing the material even closer to her body and allowing him to see its natural response to the breeze.

Forcing his gaze upward until he met hers straight on, he cleared his throat. Twice.

"Good morning, Fay."

Was it her imagination or had Adam's voice dropped a few octaves? Fay shivered and blamed it on the cool morning despite the way her skin flamed hot with embarrassment.

She'd been heading for the bath, but the need for a cup of hot tea had called to her and she'd taken a side trip to the kitchen instead, wearing next to nothing beneath her bathrobe.

A fact Adam was well aware of as his dark gaze roamed again from her crazy curls to her bare toes.

Taking a step backward, she angled her body behind the open door. "What are you doing here?" she asked through the screen.

The last thing she'd expected to find when she'd heard a dog barking on her landing was Adam, with said dog, holding a square box sporting the dragonfly logo of Doucette's Bakery.

When she'd said yesterday afternoon she needed more time, she figured he understood that meant more than one day. Not twenty-four hours had gone by and here he stood, looking very much like the rancher she'd always known he wanted to be in a starched, button-down shirt, jeans, Stetson and boots.

"What part of 'a few days' did you not understand?"

"I didn't plan on coming here this morning."

"And yet, here you are. How did you know where to find me?" Realization dawned. "Oh, wait. Your family."

"The instruction book for that newfangled java machine you put in my kitchen is longer than a Louis L'Amour Western," he said, ignoring her comment while lifting both the coffee cup and the box in his hands. "I needed coffee and I brought breakfast. If you're hungry."

This time she noticed the aroma of freshly made doughnuts as it wafted through the screen door, winning over her annoyance at being the main topic of discussion with his family. She hated to admit it, but she was famished despite a 4:00 a.m. snack of sliced apple wedges smeared with peanut butter while watching old reruns of *I Love Lucy.*

The filthy mutt sitting next to Adam lifted his snout in the air as if he too could smell the delicious pastries. "Who's your friend?"

"I have no idea. He followed me from the parking lot. You stay out here," Adam spoke to the dog, and then reached for the door handle, his hand pausing at the latch on the screen door. "Is it okay if I come in?"

Fay bit down hard on her bottom lip. Did she want him in her home? No, but what would people think if Adam Murphy was seen standing outside her door this early on a Sunday morning?

Hadn't she already given the locals enough to blabber about?

"Fine, come in."

Fay moved farther back as Adam stepped into her small kitchen, his tall stature completely filling the room. He started to close the inner door behind him, but the dog let out a sharp yelp.

"Knock it off." He shot the warning over one shoulder, then moved to shut the door again when the dog once more voiced his displeasure.

An expression of frustration crossed Adam's face, and Fay fought a smile. "You sure he's not yours? He doesn't seem to want you out of his sight."

"Stay quiet or no more doughnuts," he said to the dog.

His admonition was met with a low whimper.

"Oh, for goodness sakes leave the door open," Fay said the same moment as the timer on microwave dinged. Thankful for a reason to turn away, she took out the steaming mug of water, added a tea bag and stirred.

Adam did as she said, but when he moved to stand at the L-shaped counter that separated her tiny kitchen from the equally tiny eating nook, she moved to the far side, putting the counter between them.

"I didn't know if glazed were still your favorites, so I grabbed a few choices." He slid the box across the counter, but stayed on the kitchen side.

Ignoring the flutter in her chest over the fact the man remembered which pastry she liked best, Fay flipped open the box and lifted out a sugarcoated one. "Yes, they are. Hmm, looks like you've already had a few yourself."

"Me and the mutt." Adam jerked a thumb over his shoulder.

"You know, if you feed them, they'll stay with you forever."

Adam's eyebrow rose and Fay realized she was just seconds away from taking a bite of the breakfast staple he'd brought for her. Taking that bite anyway, she grabbed her mug and started walking backward.

"I think I should get out of this robe—ah, get dressed," she mumbled around a mouthful of food, then forced herself to swallow before continuing, "As much as I appreciate the gesture, I need to get started on my day."

"Isn't the shop closed today?"

"Yes, but Sunday is when I get caught up on paperwork, check orders, tackle bookkeeping and...other stuff." Her appetite suddenly gone, she stopped and placed the doughnut and her mug on the kitchen table. "I know you probably want to talk, but I told you yesterday I need more time."

"Fay, please. I just need to know...to ask you one thing."

The soft, almost pleading tone of his voice caught her off guard. His easygoing manner had disappeared and now he sounded almost...afraid.

That couldn't be right. What could possibly frighten him?

"I need—" His fingers clenched the coffee cup, indenting the sides almost to the point of crushing it. He walked to where she stood, set the cup down and took a deep breath. "I need to know what your decision is. About the baby."

"My decision?"

Fay had no idea what he was talking about. There were a thousand and one decisions facing her, from picking out a name, to how she planned to turn the smaller of the two bedrooms into a nursery, to figuring out a schedule as a working mother. "I don't know what you mean."

"Yesterday you said the baby was yours." Adam removed his hat, one hand rubbing hard at the back of his neck. "But I told you the baby was ours."

She ignored the quick fluttering in her belly. "Yes, I remember."

"I took your words to mean that you don't plan to— Well, that you want…the baby."

"Of course I want the baby. What else could you…"

Her voice trailed off as she understood what he was asking. Tears stung the back of her eyes. She pressed a hand low over her belly and blinked hard.

"Oh, Adam, how could you think that?" She looked into his eyes, wanting him to see the truth in hers. "Despite the situation we've found ourselves in, a lot of years have passed since we were fr-friends. You might think you don't know me very well anymore, but it never crossed my mind to do anything but have this baby."

He reached out then, his palm warm against her cheek. She jerked at his touch, but didn't back away as his fingers moved to thread into her hair. Then he closed the space between them, dropped his head and gently pressed his forehead to hers.

"I'm sorry, Fay. That was unfair." His words came out a rough whisper. "I have no right to measure what's happening now against the past."

"Whose past?" Bewilderment swamped her, and she didn't know if her confusion was from his words or his touch. "I don't understand."

He straightened then, his hand dropping away as he looked down at her. "It doesn't matter."

But it did; she could see the pain and hurt reflected in his gaze. Had there been another child? Maybe with his ex? She hadn't gotten to know his wife during his short-lived marriage. Everyone had been surprised when one day she'd packed up and left town, left Adam.

"I think it does matter."

"I apologize again." This time he stepped away from her, his gaze now centered on the hat he held in his hands. "I never should've thought that way. Weren't you heading off to get dressed?"

Fay wanted to ask him more questions, but standing there wearing nothing but a robe left her feeling even more open and exposed.

She gave a quick nod and hurried to her bedroom. The bath could wait. As she pulled on a bra, T-shirt and jeans, her cheek still burned from the heated imprint of his hand.

She should be angry that he'd shown up here unannounced. Even more so for thinking she might do harm to the child she carried, but the fury and pain toward Adam that she'd lived with for months was hard to find.

Especially after witnessing the anguish in his eyes.

Yes, she'd been overwhelmed at the news of being pregnant. And the fact that the father was the same man she'd blamed for her husband's death only added to the craziness of the situation.

But over the last week she'd found herself more and more feeling hope and joy for the future, for the tiny life growing inside her. Joy mixed with a bit of uncertainty, but that was to be expected.

Not that she'd made a conscious decision to let go of all her feelings, but finding out about the baby had changed her world completely.

Fay again laid a hand over her still flat stomach. Now that Adam knew for sure she planned to go through with the pregnancy she faced even more questions about the future.

For all of them.

Shoving her feet into well worn sneakers, she caught a glimpse of herself in the mirror, her riotous curls barely held in place by her makeshift ponytail. "Oh, yikes! Here's hoping you don't take after your mother in the hair department."

Maybe the baby would have hair the color of dark chocolate, thick and wavy like its father's when he didn't wear it in a close-cropped military style.

Fay stilled and just like that, the simple reminder of Adam's connection to Scott fanned the simmer of resentment.

Pulling in a deep breath, she pushed the thought out of her mind before it could catch hold, fixed her hair and headed back to the kitchen.

There she found Adam looking around the apartment. She tried to see it through his eyes, the space barely one third the size of his log house, but after all the hard work she'd put into turning the former storage space into a home, all she saw was eight hundred square feet that was all hers.

Free and clear.

She'd given up everything in order to keep this century-old building. Stan Luden had hired her to work in the flower shop when she was in high school, not long after his wife died. Fay soon fell in love with all things about flowers. She took classes at a local community college and found herself practically running the place before Stan passed away eight years ago, leaving her the entire building in his will.

It had taken a lot of hard work and elbow grease, but after decorating it in a shabby-chic style of muted greens, pale yellows and off-white, Fay felt more comfortable here in this tiny space than she had the sixteen years she'd lived in her former home.

"It's actually bigger on the inside that it looks," Adam said, looking around. "You've done it up nice."

"Thanks. It was a real mess up here when I started. I refinished all the hardwood floors myself, including the oak planking in the living room," she said, reaching for her now cool mug of tea. Dumping the contents in the sink, she turned and leaned against the counter. "Down the hall are two small bedrooms and the bath, which has a wonderful clawfoot tub that's still in amazing condition. It must be original to the building. I swear, there's nothing better after a long day than sinking up to my nose in bubbles—"

Fay captured her bottom lip with her teeth, cutting off her own words. "Sorry. I tend to get carried away talking about this place."

Adam's dark gaze held her for a long moment before he spoke. "It's a lot different than your old home."

Here it comes.

She'd been so caught up in showing off the warm and comfy space she'd almost forgotten who she was talking to.

She lifted her chin and returned Adam's direct stare. "Yes, it is. I guess I prefer cozy to grand."

"It suits you, but I was surprised to find out you sold…" His voice trailed off as his gaze shifted to the refrigerator, eyes narrowing. "You have a doctor's appointment scheduled for Friday?"

Fay found herself thankful that he'd spotted her calendar and the bold letters she'd printed in red and enclosed in a big heart. She was sure Adam was moments away from asking her why she'd sold her old home and that conversation was one she wasn't prepared to have with him.

Not yet.

So she went with her first instinct to distract him. "Yes, for me and the baby. Would you like to join us?"

Chapter Six

"So, that's it?" Still trying to come to terms with how fast his life had changed over the last few days, Adam leaned back in the chair where he sat at the large conference room table. The smiles on his brothers' faces eased the tightness in his chest. "That's all I have to do?"

He'd gotten up first thing this morning, drove to Murphy Mountain Log Homes and asked to speak to his brothers, at least the ones present, privately.

Then he asked for his old job back.

Even though his degree was in Farm and Ranch Management, Adam had worked for the family business from the moment the doors had opened his sophomore year in college. He preferred the outdoor side of things and worked his way up to construction manager until he'd finally led the crew that built his log home.

The plan had been to start his own ranch after that,

but the failure of his marriage had soured him on that dream. His increased tours overseas meant leaving his job with the family business behind as well. His specialty while serving in the Air Force reserves had been as a pavements and construction equipment operator. Not much pavement in building log homes, but his expertise with operating and maintaining heavy equipment meant it'd be easy for him to slide back into his old position.

Man, he never thought he'd be back as a full-time employee with two of his younger brothers as his bosses.

"What were you expecting?" Liam asked, breaking into Adam's thoughts. He stood, his dark eyes focused on the cell phone in his grip. "A blood oath like when we were kids?"

"Blood oaths?" Ric tipped his chair back, balancing it on two legs. Ric was working for the family business for a few months before continuing his studies at graduate school in the fall. "I don't remember any blood oaths."

Nolan walked behind their little brother and pushed the chair back to the floor. "That's because you're the baby. By the time you came along, Mom had already warned us against marring her youngest boy's skin or she'd tan our hides."

"No fair. I missed out on all the fun stuff," Ric groused.

"You want fun?" Bryant asked from where he sat at the head of the table. "Head out to the Camp Diamond job site and report in. You're late."

"Hey, I'm a Murphy!"

"Yeah, a Murphy who needs to get to his job," Liam added, walking out of the room. Seconds later, he popped his head back around the corner and pointed at Adam. "That includes you, too, big brother. Get to work."

Adam responded with a finger gesture that would've summoned the evil eye from his mom, but thankfully it was just him and the guys in the room.

And a dog.

Yeah, somehow the mangy mutt that latched onto him outside Fay's place had hitched a ride home yesterday in the bed of Adam's pickup without him knowing.

Once he realized he had company, a call to the local vet and animal shelter proved futile. No one was looking for a dog matching its description. At least the darn thing looked a lot cleaner after an outdoor bath revealed a coat of white. With no dog food in the house, he'd thrown two steaks on the grill.

After that, Adam pretty much forgot about his uninvited guest. Instead he got to thinking about how Fay's offer to go to her doctor's appointment, and quick ushering of him out the door, had made him forget his plan to ask about her finances.

That led to him mulling over his own money issues.

Despite his quarterly checks as shareholder in the family business and what he'd saved from his military pay, he needed a steady income to provide for his child and Fay. He wasn't eligible for his military retired pay until he reached the age of sixty.

Damn, his kid would be graduating from college by then.

"I guess turning your land into a working ranch is

on hold?" Bryan stood and gathered his reports. "Despite all you said on Saturday?"

For the moment, Adam thought. His gaze caught with Nolan's, who hovered out in the hall conferring with his secretary, Katie. "Yeah, the place needs a lot of work."

"You bet it does, just ask me and Dev," Ric chimed in as the group walked out to the main room, the dog right by Adam's side. "We showed up yesterday hoping to watch a ball game. Instead, Dev and I ended up busting our butts on that sorry excuse for a barn."

The thought of giving up his plans for the ranch had Adam marching straight to the old barn yesterday afternoon. The wooden structure looked even worse up close. After yanking on a pair of work gloves he was soon tearing the walls apart piece by piece, some of the strips of wood coming off without any struggle at all. Two hours later he was still at it when Dev and Ric had shown up. Between the three of them they'd managed to get the place down to bare studs. The foundation of the hundred-year-old structure was sound.

Now it just needed four walls. And a new roof.

"Well, look at you." Nolan and Liam joined them, Nolan punching Adam lightly in the upper arm. "Home less than a week and you've got yourself a job, a dog and a—"

"I don't have a dog," Adam sent his brother a hard stare, hoping the others hadn't noticed his slip, but the remaining three Murphys had picked up on the silent communication.

And the four-legged male in the group barked in protest.

"All evidence to the contrary," Bryant said. "I'd say you definitely have a dog, even if he is nameless. But what else have you got?"

"It's nothing," Adam said quickly. Too quickly he realized as his brothers crowded around him. "Hey, we all have jobs to get to. And no one ever said where Devlin was this morning."

"Don't worry, you'll know when Dev arrives." Liam pocketed his phone. "But don't think you're getting off that easy. What was Nolan talking about?"

"Yeah, come on. Spill." Ric offered a wide grin. "You two are hiding something."

Adam hesitated, not exactly sure why he wasn't ready for everyone to know about the child Fay was carrying.

He needed more time to figure how everything was going to work out with her for one thing. Going to the doctor's was a good first step even if Fay had blurted out the suggestion just to throw him off track.

"A date," he finally said, offering the first thought that popped into his head. "I've got a date."

Bryant gave a low whistle. "That was fast."

"Like we Murphys know any other speed," Liam chimed in.

The men laughed and then Bryant and Nolan were called away to individual teleconferences leaving just Liam and Ric behind.

"So, who's the lucky girl?"

"Fay."

"Fay Coggen?" Liam asked.

"Yes, Fay Coggen." Adam read the surprise in his brothers' eyes, but he quickly warmed to the idea of having Fay in his home again. Maybe then he could get some answers. "I'm making her dinner. At my place. Friday night. A thank-you for all the work she did."

"Wasn't her husband the guy from your unit who died a year ago?" Ric asked.

"What the hell does that have to do with anything?" Adam asked, his tone hard. "Don't you have somewhere you need to be, little brother? I think I saw your truck parked next to mine. Out back."

"Yeah, I can take a hint. I'm leaving." Ric headed for the rear exit. "You know, you guys suck sometimes."

Adam waited until Ric left before he turned back to Liam, who returned his stare with a steady gaze from behind the black square-framed glasses he sometimes wore.

"He didn't mean anything by that," Liam said.

Adam sighed and dropped his head. Yeah, he knew that.

"You sure you don't want to take some time off before coming back to work?" Liam pushed. "You've earned it, you know."

The offer was tempting, but Adam wanted Fay to know that she could count on his financial assistance right away. "No, I'm ready to work."

"Okay, then. I'll follow you to the off-site construction offices and introduce you to your crew."

"You don't have to do that."

Liam pocketed his glasses. "Yeah, I do. One of the perks of being company president." He gestured toward the stray. "Taking him along?"

Adam looked down at the dog. "I guess so. Let's go."

They left the building and headed for the parking

lot. Nolan's twin boys were tossing a baseball back and forth in the backyard and the dog raced over to join them.

Adam spotted Ric pulling out of his parking space. "Hang on," he said to Liam, who stopped to answer his phone. "I'll be right back."

He waved down his brother, glad when Ric slowed his vehicle and rolled down the driver's-side window.

"Sorry, man. Didn't mean to snap at you back there," Adam said. "My fuse seems to be a bit short lately."

"Hey, no worries. Your life has taken a one-eighty turn in the last few days." Ric grinned in an easygoing way. "Less than a week ago you were pounding sand. Look at you now."

Adam only nodded, his brother's words closer to the truth than he knew. "Yeah, I guess you're right."

He stepped back and Ric drove away. Hands braced on his hips, Adam scanned the area.

Yeah, look at him now. Working for the family business was the last place he thought he'd be all those nights he'd lain in his rack overseas and planned out his future.

Of course, being a father was also the last thing he'd envisioned, too.

A distant chopping noise caught his attention. His posture straightened and he immediately searched the skies. Adam knew what the small dot was before it had a chance to take shape. His eyes stayed glued to the small helicopter as it drew closer, the whirl of its rotors filling his ears.

He reached for the sound protection he always had on hand, but his was gone. The dirt beneath his boots was replaced with miles of poured concrete that became the flight line. The surrounding trees disappeared as hangars, support buildings and the control tower shimmered in the hot desert sun.

The bird came closer and a fine sweat broke out across his skin. He wanted to move back as the machine hovered overhead, but his feet felt glued to the ground as he tipped his face to the sky. They had incoming, but there were none on the schedule.

Who was arriving? Were there injuries? Where was the ground crew?

The questions swirled in his head as the bird started its descent. He watched the smooth approach noting the small four-seater helicopter looked out of place among the massive rotary-wing aircraft already on the ground.

The set down was gentle, with only the slightest bump that jostled Adam around his knees even from a distance.

"Pretty impressive, huh?"

He blinked hard as the machine's engines shut down. "Adam?"

A hand landed on his shoulder and he stiffened, but didn't pull away. Dropping his head, he wiped the sweat from his brow and closed eyes. A deep breath brought the familiar scents of cool morning air and the biting sharpness of the nearby forest into his nose.

"Hey, bro. You okay?" Liam asked.

Home. Destiny, Wyoming. Outside his family's business, his brother standing next to him.

Not sure what it was he just experienced, Adam was glad it was over. He opened his eyes and found the gaze of his new friend looking up at him, the animal's body solid and warm against his leg.

"Ah, yeah, I'm fine." He reached down and gave the dog a quick pat on the head. "Just didn't expect to see a helo coming at us this morning."

"I don't think your dog liked it too much. He was chasing after the boy's baseball, but then he raced to your side. Anyway, I'm glad he finally got here."

Avoiding his brother's direct gaze, Adam focused on the mutt. "Who? The dog?"

"No. Devlin." Liam pointed across the parking lot to the clearing on the other side.

Adam looked up and found his brother standing outside the bird, talking with their excited nephews. He hadn't even noticed the concrete pad before now.

"Katie called him as soon as you showed up this morning," Liam continued. "We got that baby just a few months ago. It works great in checking out both the land and our current work projects."

"And Devlin's flying?" Adam forced a smile, finally turning his gaze to his brother. "You all trust him that much?"

Liam laughed then said, "He was the only one of us crazy enough to sign on as the pilot. Dad is now talking about taking flight training, but Mom's determined to keep him on the ground. Of course, you might find it helpful in your new position."

Adam silently digested that idea as Devlin headed across the parking lot toward them. Logan and Luke went back to their ball throwing. The dog let out a low whimper that Adam took for a request to join them.

"Go on, go play."

The dog raced across the yard.

"So, you've changed your mind and decided to come back into the family fold, huh?" Dev stopped in front of him, smiling from behind his mirrored sunglasses. "Thought you had other plans."

"Plans change."

"Hey, Uncle Adam, your dog stole our ball," Logan yelled.

"And he won't give it back," Luke added.

"Give the ball back." Adam turned and looked at the dog. "Now."

Seconds later, the ball was dropped at the feet of the closest boy.

"You said yesterday you weren't keeping him." Dev removed his glasses.

"Are you kidding? That pup's been his shadow since he showed up this morning," Liam said.

"Like I said," Adam looked back at his brothers. "Plans change."

"She is such a happy bride."

Fay watched through the shop's front window as Gina Steele shared a quick hug with her mother, Sandy, and sister-in-law, Racy Steele, before the three women parted ways.

They had just ended an appointment where the flowers—garden roses in varying shades of yellow, white mums, deep burgundy ranunculuses, and orange-colored rose hips—were discussed for Gina's late-September wedding to her fiancé, Justin Dillon, Racy's brother.

Despite wearing a beautiful diamond for months,

Gina and Justin had only made their engagement official last New Year's Eve during the wedding reception for Bobby Winslow and Leeann Harris.

Fay had done the flowers for that wedding as well, a small intimate ceremony at Bobby's log mansion. She'd decorated with clusters of miniature white calla lilies and hyacinths mixed with tiny pinecones and evergreen sprigs, a perfect fit for the winter season.

Being the only florist in Destiny did have its perks.

"All brides are happy," Fay said, brushing away the now familiar wetness on her cheeks before she turned and joined Peggy at the work counter in the back of the shop.

"Oh, I almost forgot," Peggy added. "Adam Murphy stopped by and took the van. He said Mason's promised to have it back here by five o'clock."

Shocked, Fay could only stare at her employee as she continued to add delicate sprigs of white baby's breath to the floral arrangement in front of her. "He did what?"

"I gave Adam Murphy the keys to the van," Peggy repeated, pausing to step back and take a critical look at her work. "He said he was taking it in for service. You said something about an appointment yesterday so I figured it was okay."

The headache that threatened to erupt all day hovered at the back of Fay's eyes. It had been a long week, and the closer Friday afternoon got, the more nervous she became.

She'd gone back and forth a dozen times about retracting her invite to Adam for this afternoon's doctor's appointment, but the surprise and delight in his eyes last Sunday stopped her every time she reached for the phone.

She'd finally called him this morning and was oddly relieved when she got his voice mail. Leaving a quick message with the time of her appointment at her doctor's office in Laramie, she said she'd meet him there.

Now she had no ride.

"The appointment was for me." Fay sighed. "Not the van."

"For you?" Peggy turned to look at her, eyes wide. "Oh, I'm sorry. I didn't know. You were busy upstairs with the consult and asked not to be disturbed. Goodness knows that poor van could use some TLC, so when that hunky cowboy of yours—"

"It's all right, Peg." Fay cut her off. "And he's not my hunky cowboy."

"This is the same guy who's stopped by twice this week, once with fresh sandwiches from Doucette's and the other time dropping off the order from the print shop, right?"

Fay nodded. She also suspected Adam was responsible for the beautiful wildflowers stuck in an old Mason jar she'd found on her doorstep two mornings ago.

Three visits in four days, and each time Fay had been busy or out of the shop. Or not even awake yet, in the case of the flowers, which looked beautiful on her dining table.

"Well, he's certainly coming by often enough," Peggy said. "Then again, we've had a regular run on Murphys popping in this week. First, Elise to pay for the work you did at their offices on Monday, and then her husband came in the next day to buy flowers for his wife."

Fay turned away and busied herself with cleaning up the adjacent counter that separated the sales from the work area.

She'd been surprised when both of Adam's parents came by this week. Neither had mentioned the pregnancy, but she'd been touched at how each of them made a point of asking her how she was feeling.

"Oh, and Dev came by earlier today, too. He wanted to know why I skipped out on the Fireman's Bingo on Wednesday. Can you believe he noticed I wasn't there?"

That got Fay to turn back. "Peg, about Dev."

"Oh, you don't have to warn me about Devlin Murphy." Peggy waved a stalk of the tiny flowers at her, but kept her gaze on the arrangement. "He's just a friend."

"He's a charmer, and you said yourself you're still nursing a bruised heart from your divorce."

"I am, which is why flirting with Dev, and nothing but flirting, is good for my ego."

Fay wanted to believe in Peggy's smile, but she could see the pain was still there from the way her eight-year marriage had ended so suddenly last year. It had left her a single mother to an adorable six-year-old boy after her ex-husband moved in with a female coworker.

"Back to the more important issue. What are you going to do about a car? Do you want to borrow mine?"

Fay glanced at the clock over the shop's door. She needed to head out soon and Peggy needed to get over to the school to pick up her son.

"I can't. Besides, you need to pick up Curtis now."

Peggy looked at her watch. "Oh, you're right. Okay, I'll go get my little guy and when I get back you can take the car then. How's that?"

Fay nodded. Peggy grabbed her purse, promised not to get tangled up in talking to the teachers or the other parents and headed out the rear door. Grabbing the arrangement that still needed the finishing touch of a pretty bow, Fay placed it in the cooler.

The bell over her front door tinkled. Fay brushed off her hands and turned. "Hi, how can I help..."

Her voice trailed off as Adam closed the door behind him. Dressed in a pressed denim shirt, jeans and shined boots, his familiar dark cowboy hat in his hands, he looked out of place among the delicate flowers, plants and gift items that decorated the glass shelving units in the front of her shop.

A clean, masculine scent floated on the air, above the ever-present floral fragrances. Damp hair and a freshly shaved jaw told her he'd left work early to clean up. Elise had told her during her visit how excited everyone was about Adam working for the family business again. Another surprise as Fay was sure he'd focus on his land instead.

"Adam. What—why are you here?"

"I'm at your service, ma'am. You ready to go?"

Fay shook her head. No, she wasn't ready.

He moved farther into the shop, stopping when he reached the counter. "You said the doctor's appointment was at three. We should head out pretty soon."

So he had listened to her voice mail this morning. "I also said I'd meet you there."

He laid his hat on the counter and moved around the

end to where she stood. "Why take two vehicles? Especially since you don't have one at the moment."

He'd done it on purpose. She should've known. "Thanks, but no thanks. I'm borrowing Peggy's car when she gets back."

"Fay, please. Let me drive you."

As much as she hated to admit it, his gentle tone got to her. Besides, the idea of being alone with Adam during the drive to Laramie and home again wasn't as bad as leaving Peggy without a car, especially if there was an emergency. "Fine. I need to close up and leave Peg a note."

She hurried past him and locked the front door, turning over the sign to indicate the shop was closed and would be open again in thirty minutes. Adam watched her every move and Fay found herself reaching to make sure her curls were in place, but stopped herself in time.

"I'll be right back." Walking into the tiny office, she grabbed a notepad and scribbled a quick note to Peggy to leave on the back door.

Two sharp bangs echoed inside the building. Fay ran back out to the shop before she recognized the noise as the sound of a car backfiring in the street outside.

"Oh, that was the last thing I needed," she whispered, placing a hand over her racing heart. Heading again for the rear entrance, she stopped and turned back around.

Adam was gone.

Chapter Seven

His hat remained where he'd laid it on the counter, but Adam was nowhere to be seen. The front door was still locked from the inside.

Where could he have gone? Out back to his truck?

Then Fay looked down and saw the tip of his boots. Slowly moving forward, she stopped in front of her counter. Dropping to a low crouch, she was surprised to find the six-foot-plus cowboy had ducked beneath the work surface.

Eyes wide, he scanned the area, his gaze passing over her as if he didn't see her. His clenched fists rested on his bent knees. He stared without blinking.

Fay didn't have any idea where he was mentally, but she had a feeling the car backfiring out in the street had caused this reaction. She'd seen enough stories on the news and in magazines to realize Adam was suffering from some sort of post-traumatic stress courtesy of Uncle Sam and the United States Air Force.

Her heart ached for him. She had to do something. Should she touch him? "Adam? Are you okay?"

Nothing.

She suddenly wished she'd paid more attention to those stories. For the past year, she'd avoided anything connected with the military. Selfish maybe, but she saw it more as an act of self-preservation.

What should she do? Leave him alone?

She didn't want Peggy to return and find him like this. Adam would hate that.

"You know, I never did thank you for the wildflowers."

Probably a silly topic, but it was the first thing that came to mind. Maybe if she just talked to him it would bring him out of the haze that seemed to envelop him.

"I can't b-believe you still found some shooting stars blooming this late in the spring, their pink coloring is so bright." She fought to keep her voice calm and steady. "And the lupine and Wyoming paintbrushes are pretty as well, but I'm not sure how the sheriff would feel about you cutting down our state flower. I'm guessing you found them on your land?"

His fists relaxed as she spoke, his fingers flexing.

"I don't remember seeing any around your house while I was working on the yard," she continued. "Maybe they grow wild down by the riverbank?"

His eyes closed and his head hit the wall with a soft thud. He slowly pulled in a deep breath, then released it. His chest rose and fell as he repeated the action twice more.

The need to reach out to him won over her concern

as to how he might react. Gently, she placed only her fingertips on his wrist.

He immediately flipped his hand over, threaded his fingers with hers and held on.

"Adam, it's Fay."

"I know," he said softly.

"You're squeezing my hand."

"I know."

She tried not to wince as the pressure increased. "Hard. You're squeezing my hand hard."

His head shot up, eyes wide. He released her. "Oh, God, I'm sorry. I didn't mean to—dammit!"

"Don't worry about it." Fay dropped her hand to her lap, ignoring the need to rub away the tingling sensation as her circulation returned. Bracing her other hand on the counter, she pushed to her feet. "Do you feel like standing now?"

He didn't answer, but scooted out from beneath the table.

Back to his full height, he towered over her. "Are you okay?"

"I'm fine." But was he? She looked at him but his eyes seemed devoid of any emotion. "I don't know exactly what just happened. Do you?"

"Did I hurt you?" he asked, not answering her question.

"No."

"Are you sure?" He placed a hand on the counter, dwarfing hers. This time it was his fingers lightly brushing over hers that caused the tingling sensation to flare to life again.

"Y-yes, I'm sure."

She retreated from his touch, folding her arms over her chest. Her feet shifted as she tried to take a step backward, but the sales counter was right behind her.

Lifting her chin, her gaze traveled upward over his broad chest and angled jaw until she looked him in the eye. "Are you okay to drive?"

He returned her stare, his eyes clear. "Yes."

"Adam—"

"It was a conditional reflex, Fay. We've had training on the possibility of PTSD. It's something a lot of returning service members have to deal with."

"Have you dealt with any other reflexes in the week you've been back?"

Instead of answering her, Adam reached into the front pocket of his jeans and yanked out a set of keys. He pulled one hand free from the bend of her elbow and dropped them into her upturned palm. "If it makes you feel better, you can drive."

Fay closed her fingers, the metal still warm from where they had pressed close to his body.

What it cost him in male pride to make that gesture, she didn't know. Other men would've tried to convince her that what she was asking wasn't fair or reasonable, that her apprehension didn't matter.

Not this man.

Adam had put her concern ahead of any embarrassment.

"Are you parked out back?" she asked.

He nodded.

"Give me a minute to use the bathroom." She handed the keys back to him. "I'll meet you outside."

Adam kept his focus on the road ahead, but he couldn't stop from glancing over at the woman sitting in the passenger seat.

Just as he'd done several times since they'd left Destiny. He'd scared her with his reaction to the piercing cracks that had him diving for cover. Hell, he'd scared himself, especially when she'd told him how hard he'd been squeezing her hand.

It killed him to think he'd hurt her, but she'd denied it again when he asked.

In all his previous homecomings, this was the first time he'd reacted to things like the helicopter on Monday and the car today. He tried to chalk it up to all the changes that had taken place in his life since his return, but he needed to talk to someone, to get a handle on whatever was bothering him.

Before it got in the way of him being with Fay.

Giving him back his keys showed she trusted him, but he'd seen the split-second hesitation before she'd made the gesture. They hadn't spoken since they'd started out except for Fay telling him the address of her doctor's office.

"Does your doctor know I'll be at the appointment?"

Fay, startled at his question, turned to look at him. "Yes, I was actually on the phone with her when your father stopped by the shop this week."

The day after his mother had found a reason to do the same. He found himself grinning as he glanced at her. "Sorry about that. They're excited about being grandparents again. Six sons and so far, Nolan's the only one providing a new generation for them to spoil rotten."

She looked away.

"Do your parents know yet?" he asked when she remained silent. "About the baby?"

Fay shook her head, her fingers tightening on the water bottle she held in her lap. "I…I haven't had a chance to call them. They've been on a trip to Europe for the last month."

"They live in the Southwest somewhere, right?"

"Arizona." Unscrewing the top, she took a long swallow.

She'd brought three bottles with her when she'd gotten in the truck and two were already empty. At this rate, she'd be asking him to find another bathroom.

"My brothers and their families are in Scottsdale and Los Angeles," she continued, her voice low as she turned toward the door window. "Between the two, they have six kids now. My folks moved about ten years ago to be closer to them. Closer to their grandchildren."

An old memory resurfaced of the party he'd gone to the night of Fay's graduation from junior college.

Instead of focusing on their daughter, her folks had spent most of the evening praising the accomplishments of their twin sons and their career plans for law and medical school. Adam had actually been dumb enough to say something about it to Fay that night. Although she'd shrugged it off, he remembered the shaft of pain he'd seen in her eyes.

Even last summer, when their focus should've been entirely on Fay and all she was going through at Scott's funeral, her mother had seemed more concerned about getting home to the newest grandchild than her daughter's grief.

Suddenly, he desperately wanted to ask Fay to look at him now. To see if his questions had done the last thing he'd wanted to do—cause her more pain.

"The next s-street is where you turn for the hospital." The slight waver in her voice told him he'd done just as he feared.

Determined to keep his mouth shut, Adam remained silent as they parked and headed inside. Ten minutes later, they were ushered into her doctor's office.

Despite his resolve, he was forced to do most of the talking. The doctor asked about his family's medical history, not to mention a few direct questions about his past. He answered them all, feeling like a specimen under Dr. Smith's microscope the entire time. Fay had told him she'd been coming here for years. That meant her doctor knew about her family, about Scott and all that had happened in the last year.

Including how their child was conceived.

Dr. Elizabeth Smith had begun sizing him up the moment they'd shook hands. Adam found himself wondering who exactly she compared him against.

"Well, I think we're done with the information gathering for now." The doctor closed the folder lying in front of her. "If you can get me the missing information, Mr. Murphy, it will go a long way in ensuring not only a healthy pregnancy, but a healthy child."

"Of course, and please, call me Adam."

The doctor's smile was genuine and he felt like he'd passed the test. "Now, to the fun stuff." Both she and Fay stood. Adam did the same.

"Adam, you can stay here while I examine Fay. I'll send someone to get you when we're ready to do the ultrasound."

His gaze shot to Fay's, noticing the blush on her cheeks. "Ultrasound? Is something wrong?"

"Everything is fine. Fay is heading into her tenth

week and doing an ultrasound is pretty standard at this stage."

The soothing tone of the doctor's voice reassured him, but it was the bright sparkle in Fay's eyes that dropped him back into the chair.

"Did you know about this?" he asked.

She bit down on her bottom lip as she nodded. "I wanted it to be a surprise."

Adam grinned. "Mission accomplished."

The two women left the room and his grin disappeared. Other than the general knowledge that an ultrasound was a way to see inside the body, Adam had no idea what happened during an exam when it came to pregnant women.

He thought about calling his mother, but dismissed the idea. He perused the doctor's bookshelves, which contained complex medical journals. A stack of magazines caught his eye and soon he was flipping through them.

An article on how a woman's changing—and sometimes out of control—hormones during pregnancy was interesting, especially the part about increased sexual drive. Learning about the benefits of breast feeding only served to remind him how nicely Fay's shirts outlined her curves. By the time he found what he was looking for a nurse had knocked on the door.

"Mr. Murphy?" she asked. "If you'll come with me, please."

Adam set the magazine aside and followed her down a long hallway. She knocked on a closed door, then waved him inside.

He entered to find Fay the only one in the dimly lit

room. She lay on a cushioned examination table, fully clothed.

She turned to look at him. "Hey, you found me."

Hating that he had no idea what was going to happen next, Adam could only offer a quick nod.

Fay pushed herself up on her elbows. "What's wrong?"

"Nothing. Nothing's wrong."

"If this isn't—if you're not interested, you don't have to be here." She dropped back against the inclined end of the table. "I just thought you'd want to experience this."

He crossed the room in a heartbeat and reached for her hand, the same one he'd latched onto earlier this afternoon. "Believe me, there's nowhere else I'd rather be."

"Really?" This time it was Fay squeezing his hand.

"Really." He looked at her, gently brushing a curl from her cheek, his fingers staying by her ear. "You're nervous, too?"

She nodded as there was a knock at the door and the doctor entered. "Hey, you two. Ready for this?"

"Yes."

Adam's answer overlapped Fay's and they shared a smile.

"Okay, then. Let's get to it." Dr. Smith moved to the far side of the table, stepping around the machinery sitting on a cart. "Fay, let's see that belly."

Fay released his hand and quickly undid the top button, lowered the zipper and then shimmied her jeans down past her hips revealing white lace underwear.

Adam's mouth went dry.

The doctor then laid a paper sheet across Fay's lower stomach, tucking it beneath the elastic of those sexy panties to hold it in place.

Fay reached for his hand again, her touch causing Adam to blink hard and tear his gaze away from her smooth, flat belly.

"This is a water-soluble gel that allows us to get a clear view of the uterus and the baby."

Dr. Smith squirted the substance over Fay's skin. She flinched and gripped his hand. "Oh!"

"What? Does that hurt?" he asked, tightening his hold.

"No, it's just a little warm."

The doctor grinned as she placed a handheld device below Fay's belly button and slowly moved it back and forth. She turned her attention to the monitor, pressing buttons on the keyboard. "Okay, let's see if we can find…"

Her voice trailed off as a fluttering noise, like the flapping of a bird's wing, filled the air. Seconds later the noise became a louder, steady beating.

"What's that?" Adam's gaze bounced from the doctor to Fay's belly to Fay herself, surprised at the bright sheen of tears in her eyes. "Fay?"

"The baby's heartbeat." She closed her eyes and twin tears escaped down her cheeks. "That's the baby's heartbeat."

His own heart stilled as he finally understood. He leaned in closer and wiped away her tears, wanting nothing more at that moment than to kiss this woman, the mother of his child.

Fay opened her eyes.

She must've read his desire because she jerked her gaze away. "C-can we see anything on the monitor, Liz?"

Adam stood silently as Dr. Smith explained what they were viewing, pointing out the small rounded shapes and assuring them it was the baby. Fay kept her eyes on the flickering black-and-white image. When Adam slipped an arm behind her shoulders for support, she only tightened her grip.

"Everything looks really good. I can print out a couple of pictures for you today even though what you're seeing isn't much more than a blip on the screen," the doctor said, then smiled.

"Hey, that blip is my baby," Fay protested, but her tone was teasing as she released his hand and leaned back, forcing Adam to remove his arm.

"Next time we do this we'll go high-tech." The doctor set aside the equipment and turned off the machine. The room was quiet again as she gently cleaned the gel from Fay's skin. "Get some three-dimensional images of the baby."

"Oh, I've seen those pictures online! They're amazing!"

The two women bantered back and forth, more like friends than doctor and patient. He hated to admit it, but Adam almost felt left out. Other than the moment when they'd heard their child's heartbeat for the first time, Fay hadn't looked at him.

Was the thought of him wanting to kiss her really that distasteful? Or maybe the interest was only one-sided. He thought he'd seen…something in her eyes when she looked at him, but maybe that was wishful thinking on his part.

"Okay, I think we're all set." Dr. Smith rose, her hand outstretched. "It was a pleasure to meet you, Adam. I'm sure I'll see you at future appointments?"

"Oh, we haven't really talked about—"

"Count on it, Dr. Smith." Adam strong words outweighed Fay's protest as he returned the doctor's handshake. "I plan to be at every one."

She smiled. "Good. I'll see you next month."

Then she was gone and it was just the two of them in the room.

Adam turned to find Fay pulling the paper sheet free. "Ah, I guess I should leave and let you get dressed."

"That's okay. I'm just about back together here." She tugged on her jeans, lifting her backside off the table in order to get them back in place.

He should turn away, but he couldn't.

"Whew!" She sat up, tugging on her shirt. "It's been quite an afternoon."

And he didn't want it to end. "You know, it's going to be after six by the time we get home. You said on the way here Peggy was going to close up the shop for you. How about us having dinner together?"

The low lighting in the room made it difficult to read her expression, but her silence spoke volumes.

"At my place," he quickly added. "I'm cooking."

"Really? I didn't know you cooked."

"As long as you like spaghetti." He took a step toward her. "Along with a fresh garden salad and my mother's homemade sauce."

The low grumble of her stomach filled the air, causing her to laugh and Adam's heart to soar.

"Is that a yes?"

"If you include garlic bread, I'm all yours."

That's exactly what Adam wanted to hear.

"Shadow, stop begging."

"Sorry, buddy, but I'm not sharing," Fay said, then offered an apologetic grin to the dog sitting next to her chair. "I still can't believe you kept him."

"Dev suggested I take him to the vet to see if he might have one of those embedded chips. By the time we left there Monday night, he'd been examined to within an inch of his manhood, given a handful of shots and came out sporting a new collar."

Adam tried to sound grouchy, but Fay could see he and his new friend were already close by the happy greeting she and Adam had received when they arrived.

"And his name?"

"That was easy." Adam rose, taking his dishes into the kitchen. "The darn thing is exactly that, a shadow. He follows me everywhere. I've taken him to work, where he usually hangs out in the office or plays with Nolan's boys. At night he curls up at the end of my bed."

"He sleeps with you?"

Standing at the counter that separated the kitchen from the dining room, Adam's hand paused over the sink's faucet. "It's a king-size bed. There's plenty of room for both of us."

Having no idea how to respond to the intimate innuendo, Fay popped the last bite of bread into her mouth, the garlicky flavor bursting on her tongue. "Wow, this really is good."

Adam watched her for a moment then punched out a quick whistle. The dog trotted into the kitchen and was rewarded with an extra meatball before Adam put the pan into the soapy water. "Did you have enough to eat?"

"More than I should have." Fay pushed away from the dining table with a groan. "Boy, when Liz told me I needed to start putting on a few pounds, I don't think she meant all in one night."

Shutting off the water in the sink, Adam looked over at her. "You've been losing weight?"

"Morning sickness and I have been good friends for the last month." She stood, lifting her plate, silverware and glass in her hands. "Thankfully that seems to have gone away in the last week, but even before…well, you know with everything that's happened. It's been a long year."

He only nodded as he took the dirty dishes from her. Fay wanted to kick herself.

Despite the incident in her shop, his questions about her parents, and that awkward moment during the ultrasound when she'd been sure Adam was going to kiss her—

Okay, so that was pure speculation on her part, but still it'd been an amazingly wonderful afternoon that turned into a great evening. She hadn't wanted anything to spoil that.

"Why don't you relax in the living room?" Adam walked past her and gathered up the remains of their dinner from the table. "I'll just be a few more minutes here."

"You sure you don't want any help?"

He shook his head. "Nope, I'm all set. Go on, you look like you're about to fall asleep on your feet."

Realizing he was right, Fay walked to the couch and sank into the buttery soft cushions. She really should insist he take her back to her apartment now that dinner was over, but after spending so many nights alone, she found she wanted to stay.

A surprise considering her first instinct had been to turn down his dinner invitation.

She still wasn't ready to have everyone in Destiny know the two of them were having a child together. Not that sharing a meal out would lead people to that conclusion, but it would start people talking.

Then again, the locals already knew, or thought they knew, everything there was to know about her life.

Still, she was glad she'd said yes. Glad she came.

She took the light flutter low in belly as an affirmation the baby felt the same way. After months of grief and pain and anger, it was so nice to let all that go and just be...

Happy.

Right here, right now, she was happy.

Was that right? Should she feel this way?

Slipping off her flats, she wiggled her toes before curling her feet beneath her. There was still so much to deal with, her parents, her in-laws, her business, but today had been all about the precious life growing inside her.

She gently caressed her belly and thought back to

how Adam had willingly answered all of Liz's questions, even the most intimate ones about his sexual history. Her heart had flipped over in her chest when he'd made it clear she'd been the only woman he'd slept with in the past year.

Or maybe it was the way he'd looked at her when he said it. As if it was very important that she believed him.

When he'd entered the examination room and froze in the doorway, she'd thought he wasn't going to stay. But he did, and the moment they'd first heard the baby's heartbeat...

How long had she dreamed of a moment like that?

And the expressions of wonder and awe on his face as he understood what they were listening to...well, that was something she was going to remember for the rest of her life.

Would Scott have ever reacted that way?

Comparisons weren't fair, she knew that, but the thought had raced through her head anyway.

It'd taken her a long time to accept that having a baby had been her dream, not Scott's. As the years passed, and medical tests revealed how slim the chances were of that dream becoming a reality, her hope had faded to a quiet acceptance.

An acceptance that Scott had bluntly told her she'd have to learn to live with. He'd even gone so far as to suggest she find another doctor. When she tried to explain how Liz was more than just a physician and how their relationship had grown into a true friendship, his eyes would glaze over and she'd know he'd lost interest in what she said.

A trait she'd gotten used to over the course of their nearly fifteen-year marriage. So, Scott had gone on living a life filled with secrets and lies, and she'd lived hers. As the years flew by, it wasn't so hard to see how distant they'd become.

"That's in the past," Fay whispered, pushing the thought from her mind. Leaning back deeper in the cushions, she struggled to keep her eyes open. "The future is the only thing that matters now."

Hmm, it felt so good to just sit and relax. Just until Adam was done with the dishes. Then she'd open her eyes and ask him to take her home.

Moments later, she blinked then squeezed her eyes closed against the bright sunlight.

Wait, that wasn't right. It'd been almost eight o'clock by the time she and Adam had finished dinner—

She stretched her legs, then froze. Instead of sitting at one end of the leather couch in Adam's living room, she was lying flat in bed, the weight of a light quilt over her.

Over them.

She stiffened and whirled to face him. Tilting her head back, her eyes traveled upward until she found Adam's dark eyes looking down at her.

Chapter Eight

Damn, she woke up pretty.

A fact Adam had witnessed twice in the past few months. The first time was after she'd spent the night here with him and again last Sunday after she'd opened her door obviously fresh from bed. Her curls exploding around her face, eyes sleepy and sexy, full lips parted, almost naked beneath her robe.

It was the same way she'd woken up now, except for the naked part. The thought of undressing her last night to make her more comfortable had crossed his mind, but he'd only covered her with blanket instead and left the room.

Before he did something really stupid.

Like join her.

After he showered this morning and made a pot of coffee, having finally figured out how to run that fancy machine, Fay still hadn't stirred.

He came back to check on her and she'd looked so warm, so right lying in his bed that he gave into temptation.

His weight had dipped the mattress and in her sleep, she'd angled away from him, her backside pressing against his hip. The need to mimic her movement, to wrap his arm around her and pull her body close, had been strong, but he refrained in case she woke up suddenly.

Like she'd just done.

"Good morning," he said with a smile.

"What—what am I doing here?" Her voice was warm and low, almost a purr, and his body responded.

"Sleeping."

She brushed a wayward curl off her cheek. "What time is it?"

The bouncy length of hair sprang back to its original spot. Adam couldn't resist, and gently tucked it behind her ear. "Almost seven."

"Seven?" She blinked several times, her green eyes relaying her confusion. "In the morning? Saturday morning?"

"Last time I checked."

This time she groaned and pushed at his chest. As much as he enjoyed the feel of her hands on him, when she started kicking off the covers, she kicked at him as well. A little too close for comfort.

He moved off the bed and she scrambled after him.

"What happened?" She pushed her hair away from her face again. When her fingers became tangled, she yanked out the elastic band, wincing. "Ow! How—how did I end up spending the night in your bed? Why didn't you take me home?"

"When I got to the couch last night you were already asleep." He jammed his hands in his pockets. He had to or else he was going to sink them into those sexy curls of hers. "I tried to wake you. I nudged a few times, said your name."

Fay's eyes narrowed. "Doesn't sound like you tried very hard."

He hadn't.

What he'd done was wrap her in his arms, loving the feel of her soft curves pressed to his side, his hand resting against the warm skin of her waist. He'd started slowly massaging her lower back and the soft moan of appreciation that escaped her lips had him shifting against the cushions thanks to his suddenly too tight jeans.

He'd keep that bit of information to himself.

"You muttered something about it being a long week, how tired you were and to give you a minute," he said instead. "Then you fell back asleep. After a half hour of listening to you snore, I carried you back here."

"I do not snore." Her gaze flicked to his bed. "Where did you sleep?"

"On the couch. With the dog."

Not that he'd slept that much anyway. Somewhere between watching Fay sit across from him at his dining table and his morning shower, he'd done some thinking.

A lot of thinking.

And he'd come to a decision. A decision he couldn't wait to share with her.

She shook her head. "I can't believe I fell asleep like that. I just can't…"

"Fay, we need to talk."

"No, you need to take me home. Now." She righted her twisted shirt and smoothed her palms over her thighs to do the same thing to her jeans. "Where are my shoes?"

"Still in the living room. Look, I've been doing a lot of thinking—"

She turned away and headed across the room. "Excuse me. I need to pee."

"Marry me."

Fay froze, then slowly turned around. "What?"

"I think we should get married."

Eyes wide and mouth open, she only stared at him. He'd surprised her. He knew that was putting it mildly, but once the idea had come to him, it'd taken root quickly and hung on.

Now came the hard part. Convincing Fay.

"Say something."

She gestured toward the bathroom door. "I'm…I'll be right back."

"Think about it, Fay." He followed, but stopped short when she closed the door in his face. Bracing his hands on the frame, he waited. "Getting married is the right thing to do."

A few minutes later, he heard the flush of the toilet and the running of water before she yanked the door back open. "Are you crazy? Wait, don't answer that. You don't have to answer that!"

Okay, convincing her this was a good idea might be tougher than he thought. "We're going to be a family."

"No, what we're going to be is parents." She pushed past him. "Each of us. Separately."

"Together."

"One night of great sex and a spaghetti dinner does not make a family."

Adam filed away the great sex comment to mull over later. "I can take care of you."

"I can take care of myself," she retorted as she walked out of the room. "Now, please drive me home. The shop opens in two hours."

He followed, not willing to give up on this yet. When the idea first came to him, he had to admit the thought of getting married again had caused him to stop pacing and sit. Hard. But then he glanced at the blurry little lump on the ultrasound print and knew he wanted nothing more than to be there for his child, for Fay, from this day forward.

"Okay, then, I *want* to take care of you. Better?"

Fay jammed her feet into her shoes and reached for her purse. "Amazingly no, that's not better."

"It costs a lot of money to have a baby, to raise a child." Adam stood in front of her. "Why do you think I went back to work for my family?"

Fay detoured around him and headed for the front door. "I have no idea."

"What happened to Coggen Motors?"

The hesitation was so slight he might have missed it if he wasn't watching her so closely. "I don't know what you're talking about."

"Neither you nor the Coggens have any connection to a company that was part of their family for over fifty years." He moved in closer. "What happened after Scott died?"

"Walter retired long before you and Scott shipped out."

"But that doesn't explain why Scott's partner totally owns the company now. Walter and Mavis must've kept some portion."

Fay dropped her gaze, shaking her head. "They turned everything over to Scott."

"Then his stake should be yours."

She crossed her arms and looked away.

"Unless you sold it after he died?" Adam pushed when Fay stayed silent. "Why would you do that?"

"I didn't sell anything."

"Except your home."

"I didn't sell that either. The bank took it, just like Scott's partner took one hundred percent ownership of the company." Fay's voice rang low and hollow, void of any emotion as she smacked a hand hard against her chest. "I had no control, no say…over anything. Scott's death revealed a financial nightmare that took months to sort through. He'd put everything he had, everything his family had, up as collateral for loans against gambling debts he could never pay. When he died those loans came due."

Hearing rumors about his buddy's shady financial dealings was one thing. The humiliation on Fay's face as she confirmed what he'd learned in the week he'd been home was something else entirely.

He reached for her, but stopped when she scooted away from his outstretched hand. "Fay, I'm sorry."

"All I have left is my shop and the apartment above

it." Her voice rose. "And both of them are mine, free and clear. It might not be much, but it'll be enough. For me *and* the baby."

No mention of him being anywhere in that picture.

Another thought Adam tucked away for later. "What about the one-time death gratuity from the Air Force?"

She lifted her chin. "That also went to paying off debts."

Adam couldn't believe it. "And the life insurance from the Servicemembers' Group? The monthly DIC benefit?"

"There was no insurance policy that listed me as a beneficiary. Yes, I know the military was supposed to notify me when Scott opted out of the program, which they claim they did, but I never got any letter."

"And the monthly payment as a surviving spouse?"

"Do you have any idea how expensive round-the-clock care is? Mavis lost everything. First her son, and then her husband suffered a stroke that totally incapacitated him. They were forced to sell their home to pay for his care. That monthly check from the government covers her living expenses."

Her voice caught and she gulped in a shuddering breath. Adam saw the bright sheen of tears in her eyes before she blinked them away.

"So you see? I c-can't marry you, because if I do, I lose that money."

"Fay—"

"So if you don't mind I really want to go home now. I have a business to open…" The request faded as her gaze locked on something over his shoulder.

Adam knew immediately what she saw.

His camouflage uniform, freshly cleaned and still covered in plastic from the dry cleaners, hung off the back of one of the bar stools. He'd gotten it from his bedroom closet sometime during the night, along with the boots he'd polished to a mirrored shine, in order to make sure everything was squared away for later today.

"Why is that…oh, God, are you leaving again?" Panic filled her eyes as she looked back at him. "I thought you were done. Retired."

"I'm not going anywhere. My reserve unit returns home today. Their plane lands in Cheyenne at eighteen hundred—six o'clock tonight," Adam said hastily, glad to see the fear ease in her wide eyes. "I told you the day I got back that everyone else was coming home early, too."

"Y-yes, of course. I did get a phone call…notifying me of that. You're going to the welcome-home cere-mony?"

He nodded. "My whole family is, but I'm sure we have room if you'd like to join us."

She shook her head, her eyes filled with tears. "No, the only place I'm going is home. Right now."

"You know, you're dumber than you look."

Adam ignored his brother's comment and remained silent as he grabbed two sacks of groceries with one hand and put them in the bed of his truck.

"Which doesn't say much for the rest of the family because all us Murphy boys look alike," Devlin con-tinued, reaching for the remaining two bags. "Did you really think she'd say yes?"

Adam had spotted his brother as he was on his way

out of the supermarket. Devlin had been standing near the watermelons with a pretty brunette. He couldn't hear his brother's comments, but he did watch as the girl smiled and then wrote what was probably her phone number on Dev's palm.

Go figure.

"You've asked me that before." Adam glared at his brother, even though Dev couldn't see his stare thanks to his sunglasses.

"Yeah, I did. Right after you finally broke down last week during the Fourth of July picnic and told me why you were being a moody pain-in-the-ass. Not to mention giving everyone the silent treatment."

"I wasn't being an ass."

"No, you were being a *pain* in the ass and you know it. And you still haven't answered my question about why you thought she'd accept."

"There could be a reason for that. Like it being none of your business."

"Or it could be because you don't have a clue."

Adam wondered again what possessed him to unload all that happened between him and Fay to his brother. Maybe because Dev had been the only one to realize Adam had spent most of the time during the town's annual parade and picnic searching for someone.

For Fay.

And yeah, being an ass.

Dev had followed him around like a puppy dog, much like Shadow did, and bugged him until Adam had finally blurted out everything, from the night of great sex to finding out about the baby to his hasty marriage proposal.

"You know, I'm still trying to picture you with a kid." Devlin leaned forward and rested his forearms on the side of the truck. "Which isn't too hard because you were saddled with corralling the rest of us growing up, but what I can't get over is you actually proposed to a woman after one measly date? So, should I call dibs on being your best man?"

Adam sighed and wondered again what had made him decide to confide in his brother.

Maybe because he couldn't get Fay's words or the pained expression on her face out of his head. Maybe because the fireworks at the town fairgrounds had him heading home after the first colorful explosion, ensuring a phone call to the Veterans' Center in Cheyenne the next day.

Or maybe because he was hoping Dev would tell him that he hadn't screwed up too badly.

That Fay would eventually talk to him again. Something she'd avoided masterfully in the last ten days.

Not that he blamed her.

"You know you're not helping, right?" Adam said.

"Yeah, I know." Dev's smile disappeared. "Look, all kidding aside, I think you stepping up to the plate and trying to do the right thing for your kid is great."

"Thanks."

"I also think Fay is a terrific lady and you two obviously have…something going on, but she's been through a lot. Maybe you just need to back off and show her she's got your support, you know, for the baby, no matter what."

"If I ever get the chance to talk to her again." Adam dug into his pocket for his keys. "I've left messages she won't return. She's always gone or busy when I stop by the shop. And according to Peggy, she spent the long holiday weekend out of town with friends."

"Not surprising."

Adam agreed. Saturday had been the one-year anniversary of Scott's death. The hurt and pain his buddy had caused both his parents and Fay still burned deep in his gut. So bad, he hadn't even been able to visit the man's grave again.

"Look, forget about—" Dev stopped, his attention focused over Adam's shoulder. With the tip of his finger, he eased his shades down his nose. "Target sighted. Eleven o'clock."

Adam looked and found Fay walking away from the next store over, a wholesaler that carried everything from televisions to toys, pushing a full cart.

He glanced at his brother. "Should I?"

Dev sighed. "You need me to write down some how-to's and helpful hints?"

"Now who's being an ass?" Adam tossed his keys to his brother. "If I'm not back in five minutes take my stuff home."

"Hey! I've got my Jeep here."

Adam pointed to his brother's hand as he started around the end of his truck. "Call your latest conquest and ask her to give you a ride back to pick it up."

Dev brightened. "Good idea."

Keeping Fay in his sights, Adam weaved through parked cars until he reached her van just after she unlocked the sliding door. She tugged on it a few times before it finally gave way. Adam came up behind her in time to hear her soft moan.

"Fay? What is it?"

She gasped and spun around. "Adam! What are you—geez, you scared me half to death!"

"Are you okay?" He took a step closer, noticing how her forehead glistened with sweat. Today was hot, a typical Wyoming summer day. She wore a sleeveless top and shorts, shorts that drew his gaze to her incredible legs before it traveled back up to her pale face. Her outfit should've kept her cool. "I heard you—well, it sounded like you might be in pain."

"I'm not." She turned back to her loaded cart. "I'm fine."

"Fay, please. Hear me out."

"Oh, Adam, I don't think we have anything more to say to each other." She lifted a bulky bag and placed it in the van. "I'm not marrying you."

Yes, she'd made that clear, but he wasn't giving up. "Can I help with those?"

She shook her head, not looking at him as a second bag followed the first. "It's just florist foam. Bulky, but not heavy. I can handle it."

Determined to find a way to break through the wall she'd erected, Adam went with the truth. "I was wrong. Asking—hell, I practically insisted you to marry me. I'm sorry, Fay. That was really stupid."

Her head jerked up, empathy in her gaze. "Adam, I never thought your proposal was stupid. Just unnecessary."

Okay, he had no idea how to take that.

"I know you want to be involved with the pregnancy—"

"Not just the pregnancy." Adam grabbed the last bag

from her cart and set it inside the van with the others. "I want to be a full-time father to my child."

"I know. You've made that obvious as well, which means we have a lot to talk about over the coming months."

"I don't think we should wait that long."

She sighed. "Adam, that's not what I meant, but I— Oh!" Fay latched one hand onto his arm, her nails digging into his skin as her free hand pressed against her stomach.

"What? What's wrong?"

She shook her head, her hand moving back and forth a few times over the front of her shirt before she straightened. "It's nothing. I'm fine. Just a twinge."

"Fay—"

"I've had a few of them today. Probably brought on by stress." She dropped her hold on him and reached for the door handle. "I'm fine."

Adam got there first. He gently pulled her hand away and easily slid the door closed. "Are you sure?"

"Yes, I'm sure." She pulled her keys from her purse. "Now, if you don't mind, I need to get back to my shop."

He wasn't ready to leave her, but keeping her here in the parking lot wasn't right. Maybe he should just let her go, take care of his groceries and then head back to town.

"Okay." He started to back away, forcing his feet to move. "Drive safe."

She nodded and faced the driver's-side door. "You, too—Adam!"

Fay fell forward against the van, her hand again

pressed against her belly. Three steps and he pulled her into his arms. "I've got you. What's going on?"

She shook her head, her breaths coming in short gasps. "I don't know. I thought it was just— Oh, goodness!"

Afraid she might collapse, Adam grabbed her keys and lifted her into his arms. He moved around the front of the van and seconds later had her buckled into the passenger seat. Hopping in behind the wheel, he reached for his cell phone and shoved the key into the ignition.

"I need...to call Liz."

"Already on it." He punched the code that linked him to the doctor's office. He then put the phone into the cup holder after activating the speaker button. He was just pulling out of the parking lot when the front desk put him through to Dr. Smith.

"Fay, sweetie, I know you're scared," the doctor's voice was calm as she spoke, "but I need to know what kind of pains you're having."

"Sharp, jabbing." Adam fought to keep his eyes on the traffic but he saw Fay bite hard on her bottom lip, her eyes closed tight as she struggled to answer. "They don't last long, but there's a dull ache...everywhere."

"Are you spotting at all?"

Adam's heart seized in his chest as a rush of wrenching terror took hold.

No, not that. Not again.

Fay shook her head. "I don't think so. I felt something...a stitch in my side last night when I missed a step on the stairs heading up to my apartment, but it went away. This...this is different."

"Adam, I'm at the hospital in Laramie. How soon can you get here?"

He pressed on the gas pedal, inching the speedometer higher. "We'll be there in twenty minutes."

"I'll meet the two of you in the emergency room."

Chapter Nine

"The final diagnosis is officially called a partial placental abruption." Liz's smile was confident and her fingers cool when she clasped Fay's hand. "Which I know sounds very scary, but you and the baby are just fine."

Fay sank into the pillows at her back, relief flooding her. "What exactly does that mean?"

"It means the placenta suffered a very small detachment from the uterus. We didn't spot it during the first ultrasound, either because of the length or because the separation occurred in the last week or so. That's why I did the trans-vaginal ultrasound today."

"And I shouldn't worry?"

"From the location of the separation, I don't believe it will detach any further. There's every chance it'll heal all on its own."

Fay closed her eyes and breathed what felt like her

first true breath in the last two hours. Huddling in the passenger seat, trying to fight off the blinding terror that something was wrong with the baby had taken every ounce of strength she had.

Adam's surprise appearance in the parking lot had been unnerving at first, mainly because the sight of him in jeans, a faded T-shirt from Blue Creek Saloon, a popular bar in Destiny, and cowboy boots had her heart pounding wildly in her chest.

Angry at herself for reacting that way, she'd been snippy with him, but thank goodness he'd been there for her, for the baby. She'd needed his solid presence to help calm her. She'd needed him to get her here.

"Adam!" Her eyes flew open. She lifted up on one shoulder, and gripped Liz's hand. "Have you told him yet that I'm— That everything's okay?"

"I'm heading there right now." Liz smiled. "The last time I stopped by the E.R. cubicle he was pacing like a caged animal at the zoo. I think a few of the nursing students are either half in love with him or scared to death."

Fay relaxed. "Yes, he was really worried about the baby."

"And about you." Liz pulled from Fay's touch and made a notation in the folder she held. "You know, if my opinion counts for anything, I really like the guy."

Fay lay back down, releasing a puff of breath that lifted the curls from her forehead. "Yes, you mentioned that a few times over the weekend."

"More importantly, I think you like him, too."

Bunching the light cotton blanket in her fists, Fay

struggled to keep her voice light as she stared at the ceiling. "Adam and I have been friends a long time."

"More than friends. At least for one night."

"Liz, we've talked about this between pints of ice cream and a marathon of classic movie musicals. It was just one night."

"Hmm, so you keep saying." Her friend waved off her words. "Okay, like I said, both you and the baby are fine, but you do need to take it easy. Let someone else do the heavy lifting around the shop from now on. No prolonged standing and try to limit the number of trips up and down your stairs to once or twice a day."

"Do you know what caused the separation?"

"There's really no way to tell as there was no direct trauma like a car accident or a fall. We've also ruled out the usual possible causes like high blood pressure or smoking. I do plan to monitor you closely for the remainder of the pregnancy, but for now you need to slow down and keep stress to a minimum."

Fay nodded, taking all of her friend's advice to heart.

"I know you've been under a lot of pressure for a long time, but too much is not good for anyone, especially a pregnant lady. Job stress, life stress, family stress. Perhaps it's time to rethink a few things. To let go and move on."

Fay nodded again. Letting go was another topic they'd talked about during their long weekend at Liz's cottage on a lake just outside of Cheyenne.

After Adam's shocking proposal of marriage the week before and the way she'd blurted out her financial troubles, Fay had wanted nothing more than to get away. Adding the guilt that'd swamped her over how happy she'd been sitting in his living room the night before hadn't helped her tumultuous emotions either. So she'd closed the shop for the holiday and had Peggy take over for the long weekend.

Liz had gone with her to visit Walter and Mavis on the anniversary of Scott's death, but Fay could only listen to Mavis extol the virtues of their son for so long. The more she spent her days sitting at Walter's bedside, the more the woman faded into the past, revisiting stories from Scott's years in high school and college.

Except for that afternoon, spending a few days with Liz had been fun and relaxing. It'd felt good to share all the craziness that'd been going on since Adam's return, even if Liz kept pointing out how terrific she thought Adam was after meeting him. They'd read fashion magazines, given each other manicures and enjoyed some much needed girl time.

"If you have any more pain or spotting, call me right away." Liz's voice cut into her thoughts. "Oh, and just in case the opportunity arises, forget it. You're on pelvic rest for the next couple of weeks, too."

"Pelvic rest?"

Her friend leaned closer, her voice a staged whisper. "No sex."

"Liz!"

"Hey, I've seen the way that guy downstairs looks at you."

Fay shook her head. "That's your overactive imagination at work. Adam is only worried about the bab—"

A commotion out in the hall drew both Fay and Liz's attention. Liz started for the door after they heard a nurse say, "I'm sorry, sir, but you can't go in there."

"Yes, I can."

Three words, spoken slow, low and all male.

Adam.

Liz grinned as she opened the partially closed door just as Adam's large hand pressed up against it. "I see you couldn't wait any longer. I apologize, but the E.R. was my next stop."

"How is she?" he asked, stepping inside.

"I'm fine." Fay sat up in bed, tossing back the blanket until she remembered she was wearing nothing but a flimsy hospital gown. She dragged the cotton material back over her lap. "See?"

He crossed the room, his heated gaze covering her from head to toe and back again. "Really? You're okay? The both of you? I know I seem to keep asking you that, but you really had me scared there for a while."

Swallowing hard past the lump in her throat, Fay nodded. "We're both just fine, and ready to get out of here."

His shoulders relaxed. Adam turned to Liz. "I can take her home now?"

"Of course." Liz closed her folder. "Remember what I said, Fay. I'll have my office call with a follow-up appointment."

Fay watched her friend leave the room, biting back the urge to call her back. Suddenly, the idea of being alone with Adam was...unsettling.

"Do they know what caused the pain?"

She quickly relayed what Liz had told her. Adam listened intently, his only reaction a step closer to the bed. So close, she had to stop swinging her feet or else she'd come in contact with his jean-clad legs.

Again.

"You probably want some privacy to dress," he said, after she finished talking. "I'll wait out in the hall."

She put a hand on his arm—his skin was warm to her touch—and stopped him from leaving. "Thank you, Adam. For bringing me here. For being so calm and patient with me."

Adam cupped the back of her head with one hand, leaned down and placed a quick kiss at her temple. "You have no idea…." His voice was rough as he spoke, his lips moving in her hair. "I'm just glad that nothing happened…to either of you."

Unable to respond verbally, Fay could only nod. He released her and walked away. Watching him leave the room, she forced herself not to touch the spot where he'd kissed her.

After dressing quickly, she exited the room to find Adam and Liz off to one side in a deep conversation. Fay refused to admit how disconcerting it was to see them standing there together, and focused on signing her release papers.

"All set?"

She turned and only Adam was there. "Yes. Let's go home."

They walked out to the parking lot together, Adam's hand warm and solid against her lower back. She climbed into the passenger side of the vehicle and soon they pulled out of the hospital's parking lot.

Silence filled the van's interior as she watched Adam drive, noticing how his hands clenched the steering wheel so tight the ridge of his knuckles were white.

He turned to look at her just then, saw she was staring at his hands and relaxed his fingers.

"I guess we both need to learn not to be so uptight," he said.

Fay tensed, waiting for the lecture, sure that Liz had shared her list of "not-to-do's" with Adam.

All her life, that's what men did, lecture.

First her father, who never said anything in a few words, not when he believed the more he spoke, the more he drove his point home. A trait he'd passed on to his sons as the twins had often preached to her while growing up. There were even times when Scott had a hard time letting go of a topic, even after making his opinion clear.

Despite Liz's assurances, Fay was still trying to convince herself she wasn't to blame for what happened today. Did Adam believe that as well?

"Fay, I was… I'd like you to think—to consider—" Adam paused and pulled in a deep breath before he continued. "What would you say if I asked you to move into my place?"

Stunned, Fay could only stare as Adam kept his focus on the turnoff. They crossed into the outskirts of Destiny.

"I'm not talking marriage. I know that topic is closed," he added quickly, "but we both know you need to take it easy for the baby's sake. I'm sure you're already thinking of ways to do that around the shop, but my concern is you being home alone at night. In case something happens again. I'd offer the master bedroom, but I know you won't take it. The guest room is a good size and it's all done up, you know, with matching curtains and blankets and stuff."

That got her to smile. "I know. I'm the one who decorated it. All you had was a naked bed and your desk."

His gaze shot in her direction for a quick moment. "Ah, yeah, well, I can move my desk into the third room and you can bring anything you want with you. Heck, I'll move your bed if you want."

"Adam—"

"I've been putting in long days at work, coming home to basically shower, grab some food and fall into bed. You'd have the place to yourself." Adam pulled into the parking area behind her shop, taking the space reserved for her van, and shut off the engine.

His hands gripped the wheel again. "We both know what Destiny is like when it comes to gossip, but I'm worried about you, about the baby. I personally don't give a damn about what people will say or think."

Fay's throat swelled. "That's easy for you to say. You haven't been the topic of whispered conversations and pitying looks."

"You know what I think?" Adam turned in the seat and faced her. "You never deserved any of what happened to you in the last year. Instead of blaming someone else or running away, you stepped up and made things right, things that weren't your fault. That's something to be proud of."

But she had blamed someone.

She'd blamed Adam for convincing Scott to follow in his hero's footsteps and join the military. At least that's what she'd always believed, what she'd clung to during those terrifying months. How wrong she'd been to lay the blame for Scott's behavior squarely on Adam's shoulders.

"You've kept your business sound and God only knows what would've happened to the Coggens if you weren't here for them. It's time for someone to step up and take care of you. Please, I'm asking you to let me do that."

Fay wanted to be resentful of his take charge attitude, but how could she when, despite his persuasive argument, Adam was allowing her to make the final decision?

Tying the waistband string that kept her pajama pants resting just below her hip bones, Fay turned to the left, then the right, studying herself in the mirror. She lifted the cotton top higher to just below her breasts, the fingers of her other hand dancing lightly over her stomach.

Yep, Liz had been right.

Her once flat belly was gone, replaced with a tiny mound. She couldn't believe she hadn't noticed until her friend mentioned the transformation at the hospital tonight. "Well, little one, I hope your mama hasn't just done the craziest thing."

"Maybe so, but it's the right thing."

Fay looked up, and yanked down her top after seeing Adam's reflection in the mirror from where he stood in the doorway of the guest bedroom.

He'd made himself scarce as soon as they'd arrived and he placed her suitcases on the queen-size bed.

After she'd told him yes while still sitting in her van outside her apartment, it'd taken a few minutes to convince him she could climb the stairs on her own power. What worked in her favor was saying she wanted to pack a few things in order to move into his place tonight.

Following behind, he'd made sure she got inside before he headed to Doucette's to pick up a couple of sandwiches for dinner. While he was gone, she'd packed some clothes and toiletries, added a few books and a couple of treasured mementos, including the ultrasound image of the baby she'd placed in a simple silver frame. A box of plants had gone down to her shop on their way out after they'd finished eating. It'd been dark by the time they pulled into his driveway.

"You getting settled?" he asked.

Fay suddenly remembered what she'd discovered just before he'd appeared. She hurried to his side, grabbed his hand and placed it over her belly.

Adam froze, but allowed her to move his hand back and forth. She shivered at his calloused touch against her skin. "Do you feel that little bump? Isn't that neat? I'm showing!"

"Ah, yeah, that's…neat." He pulled free and took a step back into the hall. "I just wanted to tell you I'm going out to work on the barn a bit."

"Now? Isn't it too dark?"

"I'm planning on getting power out there for lights, but for the time being I'm using a lantern. Shadow will probably come with me…."

His voice trailed off when Fay gestured over her shoulder at the dog lying on the bed. "He's been keeping me company while I put my things away."

Adam sighed. "Come on, Shadow. Get down from there."

The only response the dog gave was a shake of his head that caused the tags on the collar to jingle.

"It's okay if he wants to stay," Fay said, then smiled. "I don't mind having him in here."

"You do know you're not sleeping there, right?" Adam directed his comment to the dog that then closed his eyes and heaved a deep sigh.

"If you need…anything, just yell. I'm not that far away."

Maybe not physically, but Adam had become more withdrawn from the moment they'd arrived.

She nodded. "Okay."

His gaze moved once more to her belly. A powerful longing flicked in his eyes before it vanished. He turned on his heel and walked away. Seconds later, the front door opened, then closed again.

A half hour went by and she was all moved in. She should get some rest, it'd been such a long day. Crawling beneath the covers, she felt Shadow circle a few times down near her feet before he lay down. She closed her eyes, but after a few minutes she knew sleep wouldn't come.

Not with Adam still outside.

She couldn't shake the feeling that his disappearing had something to do with her.

"Come on, boy. Let's go find him."

Grabbing a flashlight from a kitchen drawer, she stepped out onto the front porch, Shadow taking off into the darkness.

The area between the house and the barn was grassy,

but she made sure to aim the beam of light in front of her slippered feet. Thankfully a full moon hung low in the sky and acted as a natural spotlight, allowing her to easily make out the skeletal framework of the old barn.

And Adam's silhouette where he leaned against a large stack of lumber.

Shadow got to him first, surprising him. He straightened, scrubbing a hand across his face as the flashlight beam arrived ahead of her.

She switched it off when she stepped into the glow of the gas lantern that sat nearby on the barn floor. "Hope we're not interrupting."

"What are you doing out here, Fay?"

His abrupt tone caught her off guard. Maybe this was a bad idea. Maybe this whole moving in thing was a bad idea. "N-nothing. I was worried about you."

"I'm fine."

He wasn't, and she didn't have any idea why.

She stepped in front of him, but Adam turned his face to the shadows. "What's wrong? I can tell you're upset. Have I done something—"

"God, no." He cut off her question, his voice ragged, as a deep shuddering breath racked his chest. "It's not you. It's me. It's today. You being in pain and not knowing why, the fear the baby was in trouble..."

The anguish in his voice drove her closer to him, to offer what comfort she could. Laying a hand on his chest, she felt the wild pounding of his heart. "Tell me, Adam."

"Tell you what?"

"About your other child, the baby you lost."

He closed his eyes and tears stung hers as she watched an array of emotions cross his face.

"I don't think she ever wanted the baby," Adam finally said, his hands covering where she'd fisted hers in his shirt. "Instead of talking…trying to understand what she was feeling, I argued with her, begged her to reconsider what she planned—maybe it was my fault she had a miscarriage." The words came slow and he often paused to tip his head back as if he needed a steadying breath to tell the heartbreaking story.

"No, Adam, you can't think that way." Fay freed her hands in order to cradle his stubble-covered jaw, making him look at her. "You loved and wanted that child. I hear it in your voice. It's as strong as what I hear when you talk about our child."

He dropped his chin, trying to pull from her touch. Releasing him, she flung her arms around his neck, clinging to his shoulders. "I'm so sorry. I can't explain why she felt that way. I don't understand."

Fay searched for the words to comfort him, but there was nothing she could say that would ease his pain. "That's not me. Please, believe me. I'd never—I want this baby, Adam. I have from the moment I found out."

His hands held tight to her hips for a moment before they slipped around her waist and pulled her into his embrace. Then he turned his head, his mouth slanting over hers with a bone-melting, soul stealing kiss.

There was a tiny moment of shock, then she plunged her fingers into his hair, pressing upward on her tiptoes to align her curves to his hard, muscular body as she opened her mouth to him. He pressed her even closer, his hands moving up beneath her top, holding her with a gentle strength. His kiss was hurried and raw, hers the same.

Thorough and possessive and wanted.

Then just as quickly as it started, Adam broke their connection and set her away from him. His hands gripped her shoulders when she swayed, her legs barely able to hold her upright.

"I, ah… That wasn't—" Adam's voice came out a broken whisper. "I didn't want that to happen."

Fay didn't know which to believe, his words or the longing she could still see in his gaze.

He released his hold on her and bent to pick up the flashlight she hadn't realized she'd dropped. "Here, you should probably go back inside now."

"Adam, I—"

"It's okay, Fay." He cut her off. "Neither one of us expected that. And, believe me, I have no intention of it happening again."

Chapter Ten

"Okay, you've got us all here, just like you asked."
Alastair Murphy beamed as he looked around the
room. "I'm guessing you have a reason for gathering
the family like this?"

His father was obviously expecting something much
different than what Adam was about to say. He hated
to disappoint him, but he had to tell the family everything that was going on between him and Fay.

Well, not everything.

Less than twenty-four hours ago he'd screwed up
and used her sympathy over his past to do what he'd
dreamed of since he'd returned home.

Hell, what'd he'd dreamed of since that night he and
Fay made love back in April.

Having her in his arms again, kissing her, had been
incredible.

Incredibly stupid.

He'd wanted his home to be a place where she and their baby would be safe and taken care of. But after promising her that his marriage idea was off the table, he'd practically attacked her.

She'd attacked him right back, too.

He wasn't so far gone not to know when a woman was kissing him back. But when he'd told her nothing like that would happen again, she'd pulled from his touch and agreed. She'd even pointed out it'd been an emotional day for both of them and that keeping things strictly platonic between them was for the best.

Yeah, right.

"Uncle Dev is missing," Abby said, her attention on the book in her lap as she curled up on the far end of the couch. "So we're not all here yet."

"Wasn't he supposed to be back an hour ago?" Bryant asked from where he sat near the oversize fireplace, Laurie perched next to him on the arm of the chair.

"He called. He's having some trouble with the helo." Liam took a long pull from his beer, his attention on his cell phone. "He's going to stop by Zachery Aviation down in Laramie before heading back."

"Is he okay?" Elise walked in from the kitchen, wiping her hands with a dish towel, a simple cotton apron around her waist. "We can hold off putting dinner on the table until he gets home."

"He's fine, mama hen," Liam said with a grin, ducking when his mother flipped the towel at his head. "We'll be nice and save some leftovers for him."

Adam glanced at his watch. He wanted to get this over with so they could eat and he could get home.

Fay had been worried his family might hear about her moving into his place from someone else and be upset at the news. He'd tried to convince her to come with him, reminding her both his folks and Nolan already knew about the baby, but she'd had a client consultation scheduled for this afternoon, so he'd agreed to do this alone.

But the longer he waited, the more his nerves ate at him.

And there was no time like the present. "Dev pretty much knows what's going on anyway, so—"

"Hey, don't start the family meeting without me." Dev walked in, pushing his shades up onto his head. "Whew, what a flight. Logan, I could sure use an ice-cold root beer."

"Sure!" The kid jumped up and raced into the kitchen.

"You know, I can never get them to do that for me," Nolan said.

"You're their dad. I'm their favorite uncle."

"Hey, Dad," Luke chimed in as if to prove him wrong. "I can get you a soda if you want."

Nolan looked at his son. "That'd be great, thanks."

"See? I'm getting them trained for you." Dev hitched one hip against the back of the oversize leather sofa. "So, why are we all here?"

Adam cleared his throat, but waited until the boys came back into the room, made their deliveries and plopped down next to their sister again, Shadow sitting contentedly between them.

"I was about to tell them about Fay—"

"Hey, that's great! You changed her mind!" Devlin

pointed his soda in Nolan's direction. "I know you're next in line agewise, but I've already called shotgun on being the best man. And boy, have I got ideas for the bachelor party..."

Dev's voice faded and he stared at the stunned looks on everyone's faces. "What? What'd I say?"

Adam shook his head at his brother's innocent expression as the questions came at him from everywhere. He held up his hands to try and ward them off, but it was only when Liam let loose with a piercing whistle that everyone quieted down.

"Fay is pregnant." Adam made the announcement quickly, before anyone spoke. "The baby is mine and she's moved into my place."

Deciding to stick to the important facts, he didn't go into details of the hospital visit that led to this decision. What was important was that Fay, and the baby, were safe and he could take care of her.

Yeah, like you took care of her out by that stack of wood?

"But we're not, I repeat, *not* involved. So there's no need for a best man as there's not going to be a wedding." He leveled a hard stare at his brother with the big mouth. "As you all know, gossip spreads faster than wildfire in this town, so I wanted everyone to hear this from me before you found out another way."

"You've been home less than a month." Liam pointed out the obvious. "How far along is Fay?"

"Almost three months."

"How is that possible, Uncle Adam?" Logan asked.

"Yeah, the math doesn't work," Luke added.

Silence filled the room. Adam felt the eyes of ten

people on him, waiting to hear how he was going to explain this. He'd wondered about having the kids here, but they were teenagers now, or would be soon, and gossip didn't have an age limit.

"Fay and I spent some time together when I was home for a quick visit back in April. You three were in Boston visiting your mother at the time."

His nephews seemed to mull over his explanation before matching shrugs told of their easy acceptance.

"So the baby is due in January?" Abby asked. "That'll make him either a Capricorn or an Aquarius like me. The goat is usually very ambitious and practical, but us water bearers are intelligent, mysterious and march to the beat of our own drum."

"And here I thought you were all that because you were a teenager," Nolan said, then smiled at his daughter.

She rolled her eyes. "Very funny, Dad. Anyway, if you ever need a babysitter, Uncle Adam, let me know. I'm signed up for a first-aid course in school come fall."

"Thanks, Abby, but we really haven't thought that far ahead."

"So, how long has Fay been staying with you?" Laurie asked.

Adam saw the long glance exchanged between his sister-in-law and his mother, but he had no idea what it meant. "She moved in last night."

"So where do things go from here, son?"

Both of Adam's parents had cornered him on two separate occasions to ask about Fay and his plans. He didn't have any answers for either of them at the time.

He could tell by the looks on their faces right now, they weren't exactly pleased with what he'd just shared.

Old-school and family-oriented, his parents had expected an engagement announcement, but Adam wasn't about to share how Fay had refused him. Not that surprising her with a marriage proposal first thing in the morning had been the best time for it.

"We don't know yet, Dad. Right now we're taking things one step at a time."

His father nodded, a half frown settling between his brows. "Well, I think you did the right thing. Living in her apartment, with those outside stairs, would've been dangerous for her to deal with come winter."

Adam was sure his father had more to say, but his practical response was so like Alistair Murphy. The fact that he'd thought the same thing made him realize he was more like his father than he thought.

He liked that.

"You know, the smallest of your three bedrooms would make a charming nursery." His mother came to stand beside Adam, placing a hand on his arm. "A crib, dresser and changing table would fit easily in there. Not to mention how nice the rocking chair would look sitting by the window."

"Oh, I saw the cutest fabric in a store last week. Baby zoo animals all done in soft rainbow colors," Laurie added. "Perfect for a boy or a girl."

"What were you doing looking at baby fabric?" Bryant asked his wife, his eyes wide.

"Just browsing, sweetie." Laurie leaned down and gave him a kiss. "Nothing for you to get excited about."

Adam suddenly knew exactly where his mother was

heading. She'd been a long-distance grandmother when Nolan's kids were born as he and his ex were living in New England at the time. Even then, she'd been heavily involved via the phone and the internet. Who knew what she'd be like in person?

"Slow down, Mom. Like I said, Fay and I still have a lot to talk about when it comes to the baby."

Hell, he'd barely remembered what they talked about over breakfast.

Considering how little sleep he'd gotten last night, waking to the smell of freshly brewed coffee had been a nice surprise. He figured Fay must've set the automatic timer last night, a trick he hadn't figured out yet.

By the time he'd gotten out of the shower, dressed and entered the kitchen, she was serving up bacon and eggs.

Not a morning person—he barely spoke to anyone until his second cup of coffee—Adam tried to listen as Fay bustled around the room chatting about things like food shopping and laundry duties.

"Your child is going to need a room of his or her own. Besides, Fay doesn't have any family in town except us."

His mother words yanked Adam from his thoughts. He opened his mouth, but she wasn't done.

"And don't even think of telling me she's not family. She's the mother of my grandchild. That makes her as much a part of this family as anyone else."

His father walked across the room and placed his arm around his wife's shoulders. "Well said, dear." He then stuck out his hand. "Congratulations, son. Welcome to fatherhood."

Adam shook his father's hand, and then accepted best wishes from everyone as they crowded around him. Relieved that they seemed to take the news so well, he really wished Fay was here. She needed to know how excited his family was about the baby.

They then moved into the dining room and took seats around the large table. Adam hung back, popping Devlin lightly with a fist to the shoulder. "Thanks a lot."

Dev grinned and dodged when Adam cocked his arm to deliver another blow. "Hey, how was I supposed to know you only got halfway to the goal line?"

Deciding his brother had already done enough damage, Adam let the comment slide as he took a seat. He couldn't hear what his mom and Laurie were talking about at the opposite end of the table, but he'd bet money it was about the newest member of the Murphy family. Something told him he needed to warn Fay about the whirlwind that was his mother.

"Well, not to steal my big brother's thunder, but since we're all here, I'd like to make an announcement myself." Ric waited until he had everyone's attention. "I've decided against going to graduate school in the fall and instead joined the Air Force. Full time. I report to Officer's Training School in Alabama next month."

Stunned silence met Ric's announcement for a moment and then the Murphys did what they did best. Talk over one another with questions and comments flying through the air while sharing a family meal.

Adam smiled at his youngest brother, not really surprised by Ric's plans as the kid had corresponded with him about joining the military for the last six months or so.

"Gee, it's a good thing you're retired, Sarge." Dev looked at Adam and winked. "Otherwise, you'd have to salute our baby brother."

"With pride," Adam shot back.

The discussion switched to Ric's career decision and the job specialty of military intelligence while they ate. After dinner was over, Adam begged off dessert and said his goodbyes. He headed for the back entrance with Shadow at his heels, a plastic dish filled with leftover lasagna and garlic bread for Fay.

"Hey, where you going?" Dev jogged up behind Adam as they headed outside.

"Home."

"Not yet. Come on, it's time to get you up in the air. We've still got plenty of daylight left. That is, if you think the *wife* won't object."

Adam pocketed his phone. He'd thought about calling, but had sent Fay a text message instead telling her he was heading home. "Very funny. I thought you were having issues with the helo."

"Naw, it's fine. I know you've been visiting the job sites recently, but there's nothing like seeing it from the air." Dev matched Adam's quick stride. "Don't tell me you've never flown in a chopper before?"

Adam hummed the opening strains of "Into the Wild Blue Yonder," the Air Force theme song.

"Okay, okay. I get it," Dev said, then grinned. "I'm not talking about those oversize birds like the Pave Hawk, even thought I'll admit the MH-60Gs do give a sweet ride."

"Hold up a minute." Adam stopped. "When have you ever flown in a Pave Hawk?"

"A while back I dated a captain in the Reserves who flew helos. Geez, I can't even remember her name. It was back during my 'party like a rock star' days. Anyway, she took me for a ride one time." Dev paused and his eyes got a faraway look in them. "Yeah, I remember…great wingspan."

Adam didn't know exactly what his brother was talking about, but he was sure of one thing. He didn't want any details. He also wasn't sure if he wanted to get inside that bird.

Thanks to the services available at the Veterans' Center, he'd been able to get a meeting with a counselor a few days ago. They'd talked about the episodes Adam had experienced and the added stress of finding out about the baby. While a diagnosis of post-traumatic stress hadn't been made definitively—that would take more time—the counselor had been pleased with the positive things in Adam's life, like his new job, family and friends, finances and physical health.

And at how happy Adam seemed about becoming a father.

Adam had left the appointment with a feeling of hope and some strategies for coping. He'd even gotten a book on exposure therapy, a method in which confronting trauma-related emotion and painful memories would, over time, diminish their effect.

No time like the present.

He checked his phone again. No response from Fay. He wondered if she'd taken time tonight to talk to Peggy about the baby. Letting her employee know about the pregnancy was necessary for Fay and the baby's health. Adam had made a comment about doing just that when they'd talked about his plans for tonight with his family, but Fay had bristled at his suggestion so he'd backed off.

"So, what do you say?" Dev asked.

Adam's gaze was drawn to the four-seater helicopter, a necessary part of running their business. "Yeah, let's do this," he said. "Take me for a ride."

"All right!"

Adam stored the leftovers in his truck and instructed the dog to stay in the backyard while Dev headed to the helicopter, his phone to his ear. Soon they were strapped inside with microphoned headsets that allowed them to communicate.

"I told Liam we were heading out," Dev said.

Adam nodded. Dev then went through a pre-flight checklist, pointing out various items on the instrument panel.

Most were too complicated to understand fully, but at least Adam could read the fuel and speed gauges and the altimeter, which told them how high off the ground they were.

First thing Adam heard was the rapid *click-click-click* of the igniter. Then a whooshing noise that Dev said was the jet fuel lighting. Next came a whine as the engine spun and the blades picked up speed overhead.

Minutes later, they were airborne. Adam tensed for a moment, and immediately put a newly learned breathing technique into play as he waited for the old memories to resurface.

Nothing came except for the relaxing of his muscles and the wonder of seeing the earth in a totally new way.

Adam felt a tap on his arm and looked at Dev, who gestured toward the ground. He glanced down and saw the entire family out on the back deck waving at them.

"The old homestead looks pretty cool from up here, doesn't it?" Dev's voice echoed in Adam's headset. "I'm going to head over to Camp Diamond, the summer camp Bobby and Leeann Winslow put together."

"I've been there. Thanks to an early spring, we completed all the buildings," Adam replied. "They're working the interiors now."

"Yeah, but our land borders Winslow's. I want you to see how we're cutting the trees out that way. Then if you want, we can buzz over the Zippenella job site and a few others."

"Sounds good."

"How about we finish with a quick fly over your place?"

Adam grinned at his brother. "Sounds perfect."

Before he knew it, ninety minutes had passed as they covered a huge area including two job sites outside of Laramie. Nolan was working on home plans for a well-known Hollywood director, a huge place in the resort town of Jackson Hole, their first on the other side of the state. The helo would make traveling to the location a breeze.

"Okay, we're losing daylight fast so let's head back by way of… Hey, you ever think up a name for your place?" Dev asked.

"I'm thinking about Never-Never Land. That's how close I am to making it a working ranch." His brother's deep chuckle filled Adam's ears. "Maybe I'll let you come up with something."

"Oh, don't tempt me, bro. Hey, looks like someone might be in some trouble down there," Dev said, dipping the bird down to just above tree level. "Do you see the white van?"

Adam's heart lurched as he picked out the vehicle on the side of the old country road that ran past his land. As they got closer he could see the right side of van was actually halfway into a ditch. The headlights shone on the trees at a weird angle and the moment he saw the painted logo of Fay's shop he felt as if his heart stopped completely.

The driver's-side door opened and seconds later, Fay got out. Adam released the breath he hadn't even known he was holding.

"What the hell is she doing way out here?" He reached for his cell phone, but Dev was already radioing the sheriff's office with Fay's location. Adam's call didn't go through and neither did his text message. "Damn! I can't reach her."

"Hey, she's seen us, she's waving," Dev said. "We'll stay overhead until the sheriff shows up."

Adam remained silent, one hand pressed hard against the glass, his gaze locked on Fay standing below them on the road. She looked so close, but still a million miles away. He couldn't tell if she was hurt in any way, but she seemed to be fine as she looked over the van, even kicking at one of the rear tires.

"If there was a place to land, you know I would, right?" Dev looked at him. "The trees are too close and with that road only being two lanes…"

Adam nodded, waving off his brother's explanation. They soon spotted flashing lights heading toward her. The Jeep pulled to a stop next to where Fay stood and Sheriff Gage Steele got out. He and Fay spoke for a moment before he looked up and waved, then leaned back inside the Jeep.

"He's calling for a tow truck and then he's going to take Fay home." Adam listened as Dev relayed the message. "We've got about a quarter tank of fuel left, but I was taught to keep an eye on my watch and not the gauge. We need to head back so I've got enough fuel to take her over to the airstrip in the morning."

"Okay, let's go, so I can get back to Fay."

Dev landed a hand on his arm. "She's okay, Adam."

He could see that, but no one knew about the scare they'd just had with the baby. He couldn't believe she was out driving on these back roads by herself in that dilapidated van. All he wanted now was to get back on the ground and get home.

Get to her.

Like most mornings, Fay had risen early, showered and dressed. Waking up hungry was the norm now and she sliced fresh fruit into a bowl as country music classics played low in the background from the kitchen radio.

Shadow sat in rapt attention at her feet, ready to scoop up any pieces before they hit the floor. He'd been a constant companion for her the last two days, moving back and forth between her bedroom and Adam's, often sleeping in the hallway between the two rooms.

Fay didn't know if Adam normally worked on Saturdays, but it was almost nine o'clock and the smell of freshly brewed coffee hadn't caused him to stir yet.

He must be so tired.

She'd arrived at his place last night moments before he did, thanks to a lift from the sheriff. Gage had told her how Dev and Adam had called in her accident. She figured as much after spotting the helicopter overhead.

Thanks to a dead cell phone she hadn't been able to call or text Adam to let him know she was okay. The relief on his face when he'd climbed down from his truck, Shadow at his side, had brought tears to her eyes.

The sound of the front door opening startled her back to the present. Fay spun around as Shadow barked and raced across the room.

Adam stepped inside, removing his battered felt cowboy hat. He spotted her as he closed the door behind him. "Good, you're up."

"Adam Murphy, you scared me to death!" She tossed the knife into the sink. "What are you— I thought you were still asleep."

"No, I was up half the night." He gave the dog a quick scratch behind his ears and then shoved his hands into his pockets. "How about you?"

"I slept fine." Fay pulled a fork from the drawer and grabbed the bowl. "I told you last night I was fine. No pains or discomfort. Then or now."

"That's good to know."

She took a bite of sliced strawberries, Adam watching as she chewed. "So, where have you been?" she asked, after swallowing. "Working on the barn?"

Adam shook his head. "Nope. Come here, I want to show you something."

Was that a smile on his lips?

Curious, she set down her bowl as Adam walked backward to the door, opened it and paused to set his hat back on his head.

He then stepped out onto the covered porch and motioned to her with a crook of his finger. "Give me your hand. Close your eyes."

"What?" Surprised, she stopped at the threshold. "Why?"

"Just do it. Please?"

She did as he asked, curling her fingers around his. Closing her eyes, she said a quick prayer that he hadn't felt the same sizzle she did when her flesh came in contact with his warm, calloused palm. "Now what?"

"Walk toward me."

He guided her outside, the heat of the July day making her glad she'd slipped on a pair of simple cotton shorts and shirt. The smooth wood of the porch was warm beneath her bare feet as she shuffled forward.

"Stand here." He released her hand, and she felt him move in behind her, placing his hands on her shoulders. "Now open your eyes."

Chapter Eleven

Fay did as he asked, stunned at the sight before her. "Oh, Adam! What have you done?"

He tightened his grip slightly, then eased his hold and gently caressed her upper arms with his fingertips. "You don't like it?"

Fighting against her body's response to his touch, she stared at the vehicle, a cross between a van and delivery truck, sitting in the shaded half-circle driveway next to Adam's pickup. Shiny and new, the truck was a pale green color, a shade lighter than the tint of the magnetic shop logo stuck on the side.

"It's beautiful, but how? Why?"

"You need transportation." He dropped his hands and moved to stand next to her. "I've had this in the works for a couple weeks. For what it'll cost to have your van fixed, it just made sense to get a new one. So I did."

Just like that?

"Adam, I can't—I know the van was on its last leg, but this is too much. It costs too much." She crossed her arms over her chest. Swallowing hard, she forced the words past her lips. "My bank account can't afford this."

Taking her elbow, he half turned her until she faced him. She looked into his eyes, read understanding in his gaze, but there was something else there, too. Concern? No, the stark emotion shining from his dark eyes was closer to fear.

"When I saw you on the side of the road last night, the van half in the ditch—" He paused, pressing his lips into a hard line. He then cleared his throat and continued. "That sight about killed me. That I couldn't get to you. You needed my help and I couldn't be right there."

"Adam, I'm fine." She dropped her arms, one hand resting over her belly. "I told you—"

"I know I can't be with you all the time, to keep you and the baby safe," he continued, overriding her words. "But when I *can* do something, like provide reliable transportation, you need to let me."

Adam stepped closer, laid his hand across her belly below hers, gently cupping the slight swell that was their child. Her stomach muscles jumped—as much a reaction to his surprise move as to the heat of his touch—and he recoiled.

She quickly placed her fingers over his before he could pull completely away. "Go on. I can tell you have more you want to say."

"Besides the fact the shop requires a vehicle like this to move supplies and materials, you explained last night how your delivery service is a major part of your business. Not to mention how much it means to you to see someone's face light up when they receive the gift of flowers." He gestured toward the driveway with his head. "Well, consider this my gift…for the baby. He deserves to be kept safe for the next seven months."

That was some gift. And the first she'd received for the child she carried.

Fay smiled. "He?"

"Or she." Adam shared her smile. "Either way is fine with me."

Oh, how the way this man's mouth rose at one corner into a sexy grin made her weak in the knees. She forced herself to look away and peered again at her new mode of transportation. "I don't know what to say."

"Try thank you."

She squeezed his hand. "Thank you. From the both of us."

Adam's fingers pressed to her belly lightly for a moment and then, as if he'd finally realized he'd been touching her this whole time, he backed away. He tugged on the brim of his Stetson, pulling it low on his brow. She tried not to take his sudden retreat personally, not after what he'd just done, but it still stung.

"Why don't we take your new wheels out for a little spin?" He dug into a pocket for a set of keys. "You can get a feel for how it moves."

"I should really finish my breakfast." Looking down, Fay wiggled her bare toes. "And I need to get shoes on."

"All right." He placed the keys in her hand and then headed down the front steps, Shadow on his heels. "I've got some work to do. Come get me when you're ready to head out."

"Aren't you hungry? I've got fresh coffee made."

He shook his head and kept walking. "Thanks, but I ate when Dev picked me up this morning. Keep the coffee warm, okay? I'll get some later."

Fay wasn't sure what she wanted more. To take her new van out for a drive or to recreate the closeness she and Adam just shared before he shut down on her.

Hurrying back inside, she finished off her breakfast and brushed her teeth. She slipped her feet into a pair of simple canvas sneakers, grabbed her purse and paused to check her reflection in the mirror, accepting that the half up, half down hairstyle would have to do.

Back outside, she tightened her grip on the new set of keys and walked toward Adam who was standing near the still dismantled barn. "I'm ready to go."

He looked up, and slowly lowered the hammer in his hand. "That was fast."

"What can I say? You got me all excited." She bit hard on her bottom lip, barely able to hold back her groan. "About the van, I mean. I want to give it a try. If you want to show me."

Adam held her gaze for a long moment before he laid the hammer on the workbench and then unhooked the tool belt that hung low around his hips.

Fay's mouth went dry. She quickly spun around and headed for the driveway. Opening the van's passenger-side door, she reached for the owner's manual stored in the glove compartment.

"Don't tell me you're one of those people who actually reads those things." His words drifted over her shoulder.

She turned. Adam stood behind her, one arm braced against the door frame. "From cover to cover."

"Yeah, I figured as much." He grinned, then stepped back. "For now, we'll just go over the basics, okay?"

Nodding, Fay followed him around to the driver's side, sliding behind the wheel as he pointed out the rearview camera and reverse sensor system. She loved the dual sliding doors—perfect for deliveries—but when he'd opened the back-end cargo doors revealing the customized shelving unit, with its cabinets, racks and drawers, fresh tears flooded her eyes.

"You can rearrange the shelving any way you want," Adam said. "Depending on if you're doing just regular running around or if you have a big event like a wedding—Fay, what is it?"

A quick and simple thank-you kiss. On the cheek.

She could honestly say that had been her plan, but when she placed one hand on the side of Adam's face to steady herself, he turned to her and their mouths collided.

A low moan slipped past her lips seconds before his tongue chased after it. She closed her eyes and welcomed him, knowing in a heartbeat how much she wanted Adam to kiss her.

Again.

One arm anchored around her waist, pressing her body fully to his. His other hand grazed her jaw before burrowing into her curls. He held her in place and she leaned into him, letting him know there was no place else she'd rather be.

This time, the kiss was different.

Powerful as when he'd kissed her less than forty-eight hours ago, but this time there was a slow control, a slow build as Adam angled his head, deepening the kiss and twisting the restless desire inside her in a way she'd never felt before.

His hand skimmed low on her back and molded over her backside, causing her hips to line up with his. She desperately longed for everything he wanted to give, to share. Her fingers curled into the soft fabric of his shirt, tightening into a fist as she gave back, shared with him.

Then suddenly Adam stopped and lifted his mouth from hers. Her eyes flew open, locked with his, and she read his need, his desire, but still he released her and backed away.

A cool rush of air flowed between them as he leaned against the inside of the cargo door, his gaze now locked on the gravel drive at their feet.

He rubbed hard at his mouth with back of his hand, pausing and holding it there for a moment before letting it fall to his side. "Sorry. I have no idea where that came from."

"Adam—"

"Yeah, that's a lie. I know exactly where that came from, but we'd agreed not to go there." He straightened and turned away, his focus on closing the door. "Boy, I've got to find a way— Ah, look, I'll get these latched. Why don't you jump in the driver's seat and we'll get going."

Not knowing what to do, other than wanting so badly to ask him to finish what he'd been about to say, Fay instead walked away. She used those moments alone to get her breathing under control.

Seconds later, Adam climbed into the passenger seat. Except for small talk about the new van, nothing else was said as they drove around the back roads before heading for town. By the time she parked outside her shop, Fay had to admit she was half in love with the vehicle.

And right on the edge of being fully in love with Adam.

On the way home, he surprised her with the news about his counseling sessions at the Veteran's Medical Center in Cheyenne. The fact that he was taking steps to understand how his time overseas affected him meant the world to Fay. She should have told him that, but then they were home, their test drive complete.

Three hours and a freshly made pot of coffee later, Adam left the house and headed for his office, claiming he had some work to catch up on.

Fay wasn't sure she believed him, but she kept busy with laundry and dusting. By midafternoon, she stared at the open freezer, realizing she hadn't taken anything out for dinner tonight. She wanted to do something special, to somehow thank Adam for his amazing gift.

And that amazing kiss?

The phone rang, interrupting her thoughts as she pulled out a couple of steaks. Tossing the frozen package on the counter, she almost grabbed the receiver, then paused.

This was Adam's home, Adam's phone. She didn't have any right to answer. Four rings and then it stopped. She guessed it went to his voice mail.

Then the song about never promising someone a rose garden filled the air. Fay grabbed her cell phone from the outside pocket of her purse and glanced at the display.

"Hey, Peggy," she answered taking a seat at the dining table. Shadow roused from where he'd been napping in a puddle of sunlight and joined her, laying his head on her lap. "Is everything okay at the shop?"

"Everything's fine. You'll never guess who just walked out of here."

"Don't tell me you're calling to pass along local gossip."

"Even if it concerns you?"

Fay's stomach clenched, her fingers tightening in the dog's fur. She'd only been staying with Adam for two days. Was it all over town already?

She forced herself to pull in a deep breath and slowly release it. "Me?"

"You know Jackie Timkins, right?"

The name sounded familiar, but Destiny was such a small town, that happened quite often. She thought for a moment, trying to place the woman. "She works at the Blue Creek, right?"

"She's the assistant manager, but because Racy's been staying home with the twins full time, she's now the acting manager."

During the ride back to Adam's last night, Fay had asked about Racy and the babies. Gage had smiled then said he and his wife had their hands full taking care of their twins, a boy and a girl, born just a couple of months ago. "What about her?"

"Well, I guess Jackie has gone out a few times with

Dev Murphy. I mean, there's not too many ladies in this town who haven't spent time with Dev—"

"You haven't." Fay cut off her friend. "Have you?"

Peggy sighed into the phone. "No. I told you, Dev and I are just friends. Anyway, Jackie said that Michelle, one of her waitresses, just moved back to Destiny from Reno and she was very excited to find out that Dev's brother, Adam—your Adam—was back in town as well."

"He's not 'my Adam.'"

"Right, and I've got a bridge in Brooklyn I can get a great deal on. Will you let me finish?"

Fay thought back at how surprised Peggy had been last night when she'd confided in her about the pregnancy and her new living arrangements. It had taken a lot of convincing before her employee accepted that there was nothing going on between her and Adam.

Except the fact they were having baby together.

"Okay, go ahead."

"Well, I guess Michelle and Adam went out on a few dates before he shipped out last time. I mean, that was well over a year and half ago, but she suggested to Jackie the four of them double date. I guess she's determined to 'hook back up and cross the finish line,' if you get my meaning."

Yes, Fay understood all too well.

Bracing her elbows on the table, she pressed her fingertips to her lips. News like this shouldn't come as a surprise, still a dull ache rose in her chest. She remembered how Adam had stressed the sparseness of his sexual activity while talking with Liz, but that didn't mean he hadn't dated. Of course he had. Back then, they had been very different people at very different places in their lives.

Now, because of one crazy night, their lives were forever entwined, but that didn't mean—

They weren't—

Adam had made it clear after both kisses he didn't want to get involved.

"Fay? You still there?"

Pulled from her jumbled thoughts, she nodded, then realized Peggy couldn't see her. "Y-yes, I'm here, but I don't think you needed to call and tell me this."

"Are you kidding? If I knew someone was going after my man—I mean, if I'd known what my ex-husband was doing during all those long hours at work—" Peggy's voice changed suddenly, catching on a half-sob. "I just thought... Oh, I'm sorry, Fay."

"Don't be. I understand."

This was less about gossip and more about what her friend had gone through with the demise of her marriage. They spoke for a few more minutes with Fay offering to come into town, but Peggy brushed her off. She assured Fay everything was okay and ended the call when a customer entered the shop.

Setting her phone down, she breathed deeply as the pain in her chest curled into a tight ball that took direct aim at her heart.

She thought about her friend and all she was going through, her thoughts drifting from the failure of Peggy's marriage to the failure of her own. Divorce and death. Different causes, but both left the survivor confused, angry and hurt.

And just when Fay had been sure she'd worked

through her feelings for Adam, moving from anger to an uneasy companionship over being first-time parents, Peggy's news about him dating that waitress bothered her. In their conversations about the fact they were having a baby together, they'd never talked about their personal lives or whether they'd be involved with other people.

She didn't have a personal life, at least not one beyond dealing with the financial fallout after Scott's death and one passionate night with Adam.

Finding out about the baby had made her realize it was time to let go of the past, accept that she'd done the best she could to fix the wrongs thrust upon her and move forward.

To make a life for her and the baby.

A life that might include Adam?

Had she accepted his offer to move in too quickly? Due to her still-tight financial situation, it wasn't like she had any other choice. Especially with Liz's warning to take it easy for the next several months.

Shadow whimpered, as if he understood her confusion.

"No, moving in here was the best thing for the baby." She spoke aloud, to herself as much as to the dog, and then looked around the beautiful home she'd worked so hard on before Adam returned.

No wonder she felt so comfortable here, having had a free hand in decorating this place as she pleased. Playing up the masculine features of the leather furniture and iron-and-wood tables Adam already owned, she'd chosen fabrics, dishes and accessories that added color and style, turning this bachelor pad into a home.

A home for a family?

Then again, when she'd started working on the house, she hadn't known she was pregnant. Despite the grief and pain she'd tried to hold on to from the moment she'd stepped inside this place again, there'd been a part of her that couldn't forget those magical hours she'd spent in Adam's arms.

Had she subconsciously wanted to create a home with the man she'd spent months blaming for all the tragedy in her life? The same man who, many years ago, had caused her to second-guess her decision to marry Scott in the first place?

If a child hadn't been created almost three months ago, would she have found a way to move on?

With Adam?

"Oh, what am I doing?" she groaned. "I can't fall in love again. I won't—"

The sound of a car door slamming shut pulled Fay from her thoughts. She scrubbed her hands over her face, surprised to find wetness on her cheeks.

Shadow headed for the front door, his tail already wagging when three quick knocks sounded from the other side. Rising, she followed. A quick peek past the buffalo-checked curtains revealed Adam's mother standing on their front porch.

His front porch. Her son's front porch.

Oh, darn it! Fay yanked open the door and plastered a smile on her face. "Elise, h-how nice to see you."

Seconds later the older woman wrapped her in her arms.

Closing her eyes, Fay prayed the ever-present tears

would somehow stay away as she gave into the older woman's warm embrace. She couldn't cry. Not now.

"Oh, Fay, we heard about the trouble you had last night," Elise Murphy whispered in her ear. "Thank goodness you're okay. You are, aren't you? Both of you?"

The stinging reached the outer edges of her eyes, but Fay squeezed them shut and by the time Elise released her hold, she'd won the fight. For now. "Yes, we're fine."

"Thank goodness." Then she beamed. "I can't tell you how happy I am for you and Adam. After all you've been through over the last year…this baby is such a blessing."

Fay was surprised at how relieved she was to hear Elise say those words. Adam had told her last night how his family had reacted to the news, but hearing it directly from Elise was wonderful.

And bittersweet.

She still hadn't been able to reach her parents to share the news with them. Deep down, Fay had no idea how they were going to respond, and telling them about another grandchild, especially under these circumstances, wasn't something she wanted to share via an email or a voice mail message.

Fay then noticed the questioning look on Elise's face and smiled, hoping it appeared genuine. "Thank you. I wasn't sure— Well, I didn't know how your family was going to react. I mean, all things considered."

"Like I told my son yesterday, a baby is always good news," Elise said. "Is it okay if we come inside for a moment?"

Fay moved back inside the house. "Yes, of course. Come in."

It was then she realized Adam's mother hadn't come alone when Laurie Murphy stepped up onto the porch as well.

"You sure you don't need my help?" Laurie called to someone over her shoulder before turning back and smiling at Fay. "Of course he doesn't. He's a Murphy."

Fay stepped forward to see which one of the brothers Laurie was talking to, but the pretty brunette tossed a long curl over one shoulder, then held up her hand. "Nope, sorry. It's a surprise. Bryant will be right in."

Another surprise? For her? Fay wasn't sure how many more she could take today. Then her manners kicked in. "Would anyone like something to drink? I've got freshly made iced tea."

"That sounds wonderful, dear. Thank you." Elise walked into the dining area. "You know, I can't get over how wonderful this place looks after all your hard work."

"It was a beautiful home to start with." Fay marveled at how she'd just wrestled with those same thoughts a moment ago. She gathered tall glasses on a tray and placed it on the table. "I didn't do all that much."

"Yes, you did." Elise gave Fay's arm a quick squeeze, then released her to take a glass of tea. "Now, if Adam can just get that barn of his into shape. It looks like a lumberyard out there with all those stacks of wood."

A hot blush fanned over Fay's cheeks. Yes, she knew those stacks well after the other night. "I guess he's been working on it when he can over the last few weeks. He's hoping to get it finished before the end of the summer."

"I'm afraid we're keeping him pretty busy at work," Laurie said, taking a glass for herself. "He might have to hire the family business to finish the job."

"Or maybe we should have an old-fashioned barn-raising and help him ourselves," Elise said, then smiled. "You know, like in that old musical with all those brothers looking for brides."

"Oh, I just watched that movie last weekend with a friend," Fay chimed in. "It was wonderful."

"Well, we certainly have enough Murphy brothers," Bryant added as he popped his head inside the front door. "Laurie, can you give me a hand by making sure this stays open? That is, if you're ready, Mom?"

Elise set down her tea. "Yes, please bring it in."

"Bring what in?" Fay asked.

Before Adam's mother could answer, Laurie hurried to hold the door and Bryant walked in carrying a gorgeous rocking chair. Dark-reddish-brown in color, the chair was tall with a curved back, flat spindles and rolled arms.

"Any special place I should put this?" Bryant asked. "It's kind of heavy."

"Why don't you take it back to the guest room?" Elisa said. "Is that all right with you, Fay?"

Stunned, Fay could only nod as Bryant headed down the hall with Shadow leading the way. The ladies followed, Fay silently thankful that she'd left the bedroom neat and tidy.

Bryant placed the rocker in the far corner near the

window, then stood back next to his wife. "Still looks pretty good for being over a hundred years old."

"A hundred and twenty-seven to be exact," Elise said, turning to face Fay. "All hand-carved in Irish oak. Alistair's great-grandmother brought it over from Ireland in the late 1880s. It's been sitting in our bedroom all these years, but now it's yours."

A powerful yearning to be deserving of such a gift welled deep inside her. Staring at the family heirloom, Fay pressed her fingers to her trembling lips as she searched for her voice.

"Elise, you sh-shouldn't have done this," she finally rasped.

"Of course I should have." Adam's mother waved off her protest. "It's a tradition in the Murphy family that this chair goes to the firstborn when a new baby is on the way. That's how Al and I came to own it when I was pregnant with Adam. And now it belongs to you."

"But I'm not—" The tears she'd managed to hold off broke free, turning her vision into a watery mess. "I can't accept this. I'm not family."

"Of course you are, dear."

At the woman's heartfelt words, Fay hung her head, covering her eyes with both hands. Moments later, she sat at the edge of the bed wrapped once again in the warm embrace of Adam's mother.

"I'm sorry." She brushed at her cheeks. Flushed hot from her lack of control, Fay kept her gaze centered on her lap. "I don't know why your generosity affected me that way."

"Oh, I remember the tears," Elise said softly, pressing tissues into Fay's hands. "Happy ones, sad ones or tears for no reason at all."

Fay looked up, but found Laurie and Bryant had left the room. Her gaze settled again on the beautiful piece of furniture. The image of sitting there, rocking contentedly over the coming months, sprang to life so easily. And after the baby arrived, she pictured walking in and finding Adam holding their child against the width of his chest.

The waterworks started again. "Oh, look at me. I'm so embarrassed."

"Don't be. Tears are one of the many joys of pregnancy." Adam's mother gave her one more squeeze before dropping her arm and instead taking Fay's hands in hers. "And happy tears are always better when shared."

Fay pulled in a deep breath, then slowly let it out. She turned and looked at the older woman sitting next to her. "You are an amazing woman, Elise Murphy. Has anyone ever told you that?"

"On a good day?" Elise winked at her. "My husband, if he's smart."

"No, I really mean it." Fay smiled as she wiped away the last of her tears. "You've raised a terrific family, created a successful business with your husband and headed more charity events in this town than I can name. Now here you are, welcoming me into your family when you could've easily—"

"Oh, stop. You're making me sound like a saint and believe me, I've got my faults." Elise released her and folded her hands primly in her lap. "Ask any of my boys and they'll tell you my number-one imperfection is that

I can't seem to mind my own business, which I'm about to prove right now."

"I don't understand."

Elise looked into her face, eyes searching hers. "Fay, are you in love with my son?"

Chapter Twelve

"And as if finding out Mom had brought over the rocking chair wasn't enough of a surprise," Adam paused to take a swallow of his lukewarm coffee while watching his brother's expression. "I found the two of them, in the bedroom, and right away I knew Fay had been crying."

Devlin had been out of town for the last couple of weeks on business, so when he'd invited Adam to meet this morning for breakfast at Sherry's Diner, Adam had agreed.

Not that he wasn't anxious to get home. Especially now that he had what he'd come into town for.

It was a beautiful Saturday morning and after spending most of his free time working on the barn, he was ready to get back to it. Two of the four walls were framed and ready to be lifted into place. Today he planned to get started on the remaining two before the pre-fabricated roof was delivered the beginning of next month.

It was amazing how banging nails eased his frustration.

Not that Adam believed that, but maybe if he said it often enough, and stayed as far away as he could from Fay, it might come true.

"And this all happened the day after you told everyone about the baby?" Dev asked.

Adam nodded. "And asked Mom not to go crazy."

"Yeah, you should've known that wasn't going to stop her," Dev said. "Did you ask why Fay was crying?"

"Of course I asked why. Both of them said they were just 'happy tears' and nothing was wrong." Adam set down his mug. "Which was a relief, actually. My first thought had been Fay was upset about the kiss."

"You kissed her?"

Adam sighed. Dammit, he hadn't meant to say that aloud.

"Well, it's about time," Dev said, then grinned. "You do realize you're doing all of this a bit backward? I mean, first comes the baby, then a marriage proposal, then a kiss?"

"Lay off, Dev."

"No, no, it's cool. You know me. I'm all for kissing… and other stuff."

"There was no other stuff."

"Oh." The gleam faded from Dev's eyes. "So what did Fay do when you kissed her?"

"Well, the first time—"

"Hold up! The first time? Okay, seeing how none of this is really any of my business, let's get to the real question. What was the lady's reaction?" Dev leaned forward, his voice low. "Did she back away? Smack you across the face? Crush your instep with the pointy end of her high heels?"

Adam stared hard at his younger brother. "Speaking from personal experience?"

"Hey, we're talking about you, not me." Dev laid a hand across his chest. "My stories are too numerous and would probably scar you for life."

Adam snorted and shook his head. "I'm sure you're right about that, but no, Fay didn't do any of those things. I'm…I'm the one who ended things. You know, before it went too far."

Dev slumped back against the booth. "Why?"

"Well, for one thing, I don't think we could have had sex—even if we both wanted to—for medical reasons." Adam quickly filled his brother in on the scare they'd had a couple of weeks ago with the baby. "And no, I didn't ask if sex was off-limits, but when the doc said for Fay to take it easy on stairs and no heavy lifting, I figured it was another one of the rules."

"But Fay and the baby are okay?"

His brother's concern touched him. Adam forced a smile and tried to keep the worry from his voice. "Yeah, they're fine."

"So, you do know that kissing can lead to…more kissing. And other stuff. Besides sex."

"Yes, you idiot, but that doesn't matter."

"Then you're not doing it right," Dev deadpanned.

Adam leaned forward. "It doesn't matter because being with me isn't what Fay wants."

"And how do you know that?"

"Because less than three months ago she hated my guts." Adam shoved the plate in front of him off to one side. Geez, putting that into words really hit home at how stupid his secret meeting early this morning had been.

Not that he couldn't change his mind, but he didn't want to. He wanted Fay.

Adam then realized Dev had stayed silent, for once, so he continued. "She blamed me for Scott being killed because he followed in my footsteps, joined the Reserves and finally got himself shipped overseas."

"When did she tell you that?"

"Back in April. The night she showed up at my place. The night we…"

"Seems she didn't hate you too much that night."

Adam sighed and sat upright again. Shoving his hands into the pockets of his denim jacket, he jammed his fingers against the small object tucked in there.

Fay had needed someone to direct her anger toward, he understood that, even more so after she'd confirmed the rumors he'd heard about the financial mess Scott had left her.

"Okay, I get that she needed to be angry with someone. I've heard the rumors, same as everyone, about her money issues." Dev reached for his coffee mug. "But hasn't she worked through all that? I mean, she's living with you, there's some physical stuff going on…is she enjoying all that as much as you?"

Adam had jumped to the same conclusions, trying to convince himself Fay was ready to move on, but he still wasn't sure. He didn't want to push her. The memories of what had led to losing his child years ago, and the uncertain physical condition Fay was currently in, made him even more determined to do what was best. Shutting down his needs, his wants, and putting Fay and the baby first would ensure they stayed safe and healthy.

At least for the time being. Who knew, maybe someday…

When his brother offered a tilt of his head and an arched brow, Adam realized he'd been waiting for an answer.

He thought back to what Dev had asked. "Yeah, she seemed to be…enjoying herself."

"So? Go for it. I mean, once you've cleared up the medical question. Hey, you're both single, living under the same roof, you've obviously spent some quality time together in the past." Dev took a quick swallow. "You know, you don't have to be in love to— Oh, wait, that's it!"

Adam remained silent, but he didn't turn away from his brother's incredulous stare.

"You're in love with her?"

Before he could decide if it was the right thing to do or not, Adam pulled his hand from his pocket and deposited a small velvet box on the table.

Dev let loose a low whistle and reached for the box. Flipping it open, he angled it toward the light, the sunshine reflecting off the large square-cut diamond tucked inside. "Wow, that's a big piece of ice. Looks like it should have a highball wrapped around it." Dev looked up. "When did you get this?"

"Early this morning. Before I met you."

"You know, buying a diamond ring from a local jeweler isn't exactly the best way to stay off the gossip grapevine."

"Actually, things have been pretty quiet where the town's busybodies are concerned. A few people have said something about us living together to Mom, of course."

Adam didn't mention his phone call with Fay's father three nights ago. The older man's not-so-subtle suggestion they wed had nothing to do with Adam's decision to do things the right way this time.

He took the box back, snapped the lid closed and put it away. "Anyway, Mr. Ryan and I had a private one-on-one meeting before his store opened. He knows how to keep a secret."

"When do you plan on getting down on one knee? Again?"

"I didn't get down the first time and I don't know when. When the moment is right."

"Which might be sooner than you think."

Adam didn't hear what his brother had mumbled behind his coffee mug. Not that it mattered. He probably shouldn't have showed him the ring anyway.

"Hey, you're going to keep this to yourself, right?" he asked.

"Yeah, sure."

Not entirely convinced, but having no other choice, Adam grabbed some bills from his wallet and tossed them on the table. "I've got to get going. It's going to be a nice day and I want to spend it working outside."

Dev set down the mug and glanced at his watch. "Ah, yeah…how about giving me a lift? I'll stick around and help."

"Where's your Jeep?"

"I walked to the diner this morning from a friend's place."

A lady friend most likely. "Fine, I could always use an extra set of hands."

They headed outside and got into Adam's pickup. Ten minutes later they took the turn out to his place. After rounding the last corner, they came across a group of vehicles parked in the open field just before his driveway.

"What's going on?" Adam asked.

Dev shrugged. "Got me."

Easing up on the gas, Adam slowed his truck and took a closer look. He easily picked out the cars and trucks belonging to his family, but he couldn't place the other ones. Then he saw the Jeep with the sheriff's emblem on the door on the side of the road and hit the gas.

"Adam, wait. Don't go nuts."

"The sheriff is at my home, along with most of our family." He swung his truck into the driveway, hit the brakes and cut the engine. "Something must be... What in the world?"

Staring through the windshield, he saw a crowd of people gathered in the yard. He looked over at Dev, who only grinned and got out the passenger side. He did the same from his side of the truck as Fay stepped down from the covered porch and headed across the yard to him.

"Are you okay?" He hurried toward her. Then, becoming aware of so many eyes on them, he stopped and yanked off his sunglasses. "I saw the sheriff's Jeep as we drove up. I got worried."

"Oh, Adam, I'm sorry." Fay joined him, the front end of his truck now between them and the crowd. "The last thing I wanted was for you to worry."

A gentle morning breeze lifted her curls and sent a sweet flowery scent in his direction. By now he recognized it as a combination of the shower wash and lotion she used on a daily basis. He couldn't walk past the hall bathroom in the mornings without the smell taking root inside his head for the rest of the day.

Damn, just the sight of her standing there in a dress that left her arms and legs bare, combined with the topic of discussion between him and Dev this morning, and Adam's traitorous body ignored his silent command not to respond. He had to take a step back, even angling his lower half toward the truck to keep her from seeing his lack of control.

"Please don't worry, I'm fine." Her voice dropped to a low whisper. "I didn't mean to—I never thought... boy, I really messed this up."

Now he was totally confused. "Messed up what?"

"You've been working so hard lately. I know how much you wanted the barn completed," she turned, waving at the group of men gathered around his make-shift workbench. "So I pulled together an old-fashioned barn-raising."

Adam looked again at the people in his yard, easily picking out his father, brothers and most of the guys from his work crew. The sheriff stood nearby talking with a younger man that looked so much like him Adam guessed it must be his brother, Garrett. Walking up to join them was the sheriff's brother-in-law, Justin, and the little boy next to him, already decked in a miniature hard hat, had to be Justin's son.

Checking out the work he'd accomplished so far was local rancher Landon Cartwright and a couple of older men who probably worked for Cartwright out at his place. Bobby Winslow and the man whose home Adam's crew was working on now, Dean Zippenella, rounded out the crowd.

He turned back to her. "How did you get all these people here?"

"Well, your mother helped. We started with your family, of course, then made a few phone calls and it sort of snowballed from there."

Fay's smile turned genuine again and Adam suddenly felt too warm inside his jacket. He wanted to take it off, but fear of dropping the precious cargo in his pocket had him standing perfectly still.

"A lot of the ladies wanted to be involved, too," she continued, her words coming in a rush. "Some might even pitch in with the manual labor. Bobby's wife, Leeann, came with her own tool belt and she and Gina already have Abby fascinated with a Sawzall, whatever that is."

She pointed toward a group of tables gathered beneath a cluster of trees. "Laurie's here, of course, and even Katie wanted to help. Racy and Maggie brought the babies as well as the older kids, so the rest of us plan to stay busy with keeping them out of the way. Later on, we're having a potluck dinner to feed everyone."

Stunned, Adam could only stare at the woman who'd

finally seemed to have run out of words. "You did all this? For me?"

Fay nodded, inching a step closer to him. "I know you dreamed of making this a working ranch. That's all changed now, thanks to the baby, but you've said how much you want to at least have horses to take care of and enjoy. I wanted to do what I could to make that happen."

"It looks like you've got half the town here." Following her lead, Adam took two steps and stood right in front of her, loving how her eyes lit up as she smiled at him. "You're not worried about how this is going to look to everyone?"

"Everyone knows we're living together, Adam." She lowered her voice. "After today, I'll give it to sundown before the news of the baby reaches the town limits."

Confusion gave way to a glimmer of hope. "And that's okay with you?"

"More than okay."

Before he knew what she was doing, Fay stepped even closer, wrapped her arms around his neck and drew his mouth down to hers for the sweetest kiss he'd ever received.

"That was some kiss."

Fay blushed. She'd been teased all afternoon, all in good fun, by everyone. She still didn't know what made her step forward and put on such a display, but the way Adam had looked at her, with such hope in his eyes... Hope and maybe something more? Or was that just wishful thinking on her part?

"It was very chaste," she finally said when she realized Liz was waiting for a response. "Just a simple kiss."

"Yeah, until your man wrapped his arms around you."

"Even then."

"Yes, but everyone—well, everyone over the age of eighteen at least—could tell he, and you, wanted it to be more. Thanks to your audience Adam behaved himself. That's what made it so sexy."

"Liz!"

"So are you ready to admit you're in love with him?"

That got her attention. Fay looked up from where she'd been staring at the remains of her lunch. She opened her mouth, but nothing came out.

"Stunned into silence?" Liz finished off the last of the pasta salad before she spoke. "Or maybe you didn't hear me the first time. Are you in love with Adam?"

"Shh!" Fay looked around, glad to see no one was close enough to hear her friend's question. "How can you ask me that?"

"Very easily. Watch, I'll do it again. Are you in love with Adam?"

"I…I can't answer that."

"Can't? Or won't?" Liz leaned in close. "You told me how you babbled your way out of answering his mother, but now that you've had time to think it over…"

"I'm still thinking it over…"

"Well, if I get a vote—"

Fay smiled. "You don't."

"But if I did, I'd say go for it. I told you when you moved in that I thought the two of you together was a good idea."

"For the health of the baby."

"For you *and* the baby. I watched how Adam looked at you during the ultrasound, at the hospital after that scare you had and again at the follow-up appointment just this past Monday. The man is crazy about you."

Fay desperately wanted to believe that, but the distance between them ever since the morning he'd given her the new van, and that second amazing kiss, told her otherwise. "He's worried about me, about the baby. Everything he's done has been for this child."

"And that includes buying you a new van, making a late-night run for microwave popcorn because you suddenly had a craving while watching reruns of *I Love Lucy* and replacing the shelving units in the shop's storeroom?" Liz ticked off the things Adam had shared during the last appointment. "All chores he relayed with much affection if I remember correctly."

Yes, Adam had done all those things, and more, in the last two weeks since she'd moved into his home.

"Oh, I didn't tell you that Adam arranged a video call to London so I could finally tell my folks about the baby."

"Wow. How did that go?"

"They said they were happy for me," Fay said, then sighed, remembering how strained the live chat had been, filled with long silences and tense words. "My mother knows how much I've longed for a child, but a pregnancy outside of marriage isn't something they approve of. I have a feeling my father pointed out that fact to Adam when they spoke privately afterward on the phone."

"Don't tell me a modern-day version of a shotgun wedding was suggested?"

"I don't know, Adam didn't say when I asked what they talked about. We were late for dinner at his parents that same night so instead of pressing for details…"

Her friend easily filled in the end of Fay's sentence. "You let it go."

"We had such a great time with them. Dev and Liam weren't there, but Nolan's kids are great, and Laurie showed me a baby blanket she's knitting for this little one." Fay patted the swell beneath the cotton material of her sundress. "They've all been so wonderful about all of this."

"Adam's been wonderful."

Yes, he has.

Despite the emotional and physical distance Adam had put between them the last couple of weeks, moving in here allowed Fay to get to know him in a way she hadn't before.

Adam was a good man, a fact she'd been aware of since their youth, but now…

She'd witnessed firsthand the respect and love he had for his parents and the playful teasing between him and his brothers. He made sure to include her, making her a part of all they shared, something that had always been missing between her and her distant family.

Yes, he'd been working long hours, both at his job and when he came home at night, but he'd been nothing but sweet and caring to her. She wasn't used to someone putting her wants and needs ahead of his own, but it was glorious to feel this way.

She was in love with him.

Her feelings for the father of her child were as simple as that kiss, and as complicated.

"Oh, Liz, what am I going to do?"

Her friend reached out and took Fay's hand. "Be happy. You both deserve to be very, very happy."

The barn was finally finished at sunset.

Their friends had started to leave a few hours earlier, with both Adam and Fay offering their heartfelt thanks for all their help, until it was just the Murphy brothers putting on the finishing touches. Even the roof was complete thanks to Adam's dad arranging to have the prebuilt frame delivered earlier in the day.

The sight of the six brothers, working side by side so far off the ground, had Fay's heart in her throat the whole time. Her gaze was locked on Adam most of the time as he gingerly moved across the roof.

Even thinking about it now, up to her nose in bubbles, caused an all too familiar ache to take root deep inside her.

If something should ever happened to Adam…

No, stop it!

Fay refused to allow her mind to go down that road. She wasn't going to live with that fear again.

Once his family had started to depart, she'd shared hugs with them all and then told Adam she wanted to head inside and relax.

What she didn't tell him was that relaxing included a long soak in a bubble bath.

In his tub.

Oh, she hoped she was doing the right thing.

A tiny voice inside her had been shouting all day

that Adam wanted to be with her, wanted to make love to her, but surprising him like this…

What if he turned her down?

Turned away from her?

Fay wasn't sure she could live with the humiliation.

Movement on the other side of the door that led to his bedroom pulled her from her thoughts, causing Fay to sink even lower into the warm, soapy water.

From her vantage point, she watched Adam sit down on to the edge of his bed, exhaustion evident from his posture as he kicked of his work boots and then leaned down to peel off his socks.

Seconds later, he reached behind his head and removed his sweat-soaked shirt, before arching and twisting his back. A low moan filled the air and Fay honestly didn't know if it was from him or her.

He hadn't looked this way so it must've been from him.

How could he not notice the light in his bathroom?

Oh, maybe this hadn't been such a good idea. Maybe after all the hard work he'd put in today, all he wanted was a hot shower.

Fay closed her eyes against the visual image her thoughts created. Adam's bathroom had a separate glass-enclosed shower right next to the tub. She easily pictured him standing there, beneath the spray, watching her watch him—

"Fay?"

The sound of him saying her name made her eyes fly open.

Adam stood in the doorway, wearing nothing but his jeans and barely that, as he'd already undone the top few buttons causing the waistband to slip low on his hips.

She couldn't stop her gaze from wandering over the length of his toned muscular body. Ripples of wanton desire coursed through her. There was a fluttering low in her belly that had nothing to do with the baby and everything to do with the baby's father.

"Fay, what are you doing in here?"

She said the first thing that popped into her head. "Taking a bath."

The corner of his mouth slowly rose into a half smile. "Yes, I can see that."

"You told me I could use your tub anytime I wanted."

He took a step toward her. "Yeah, I did say that."

Pulling in a deep breath, Fay slowly straightened her legs beneath the water, pushing herself back to the far edge of the expansive tub. Her shoulders rose above the bubbles and Adam's gaze moved hungrily over her wet, bare skin.

She wanted this moment, this man, more than she'd ever wanted anything in her entire life. All she had to do was find the strength to let him know.

"You're looking a little dirty yourself," she said.

His laugh came out in a low rasp as he brushed one large hand over the hard ridge of his stomach. "Yeah, well, I've been working hard today."

Swallowing hard to get rid of the lump in her throat, Fay lifted a hand from the water. "I know. I don't mind sharing if you'd like to join me."

Chapter Thirteen

Adam was dreaming. He had to be. There was no other explanation for what was happening at this very moment. Then again, it'd been a day of dreams coming true for him.

First, the rightness he felt deep in his gut when he'd picked up the diamond ring he was sure Fay would someday wear on her finger. Then to come home and find himself surrounded by family and friends, all working together for one goal, thanks to the beautiful woman soaking in a bubble bath right in front of him.

The moment Fay had stepped into his arms this morning, not caring that half the town had been watching, had filled him with such a powerful emotion, he was still struggling hours later to put a name to it.

Love just didn't seem strong enough.

He looked at her, her shoulders and upper arms wet and gleaming, the swell of her breasts just barely visible through the mounds of bubbles. She'd piled her hair on top of her head, but a few strands laid loose and damp, clinging to her neck. Her hands glided back and forth, moving the soapy white froth around enough that he caught a glimpse of her beautiful curves beneath the water.

Was she really offering what he hoped she was? What he'd dreamed of from the moment he'd returned and found her here inside his home?

"Adam?"

Fay's soft voice broke into his thoughts. His gaze flew back to her face in time to see a flicker of emotion reflected in her eyes before she looked away, her hand falling back into the water with a splash.

He had no idea how far this moment was going to go, but he wanted desperately to believe in the desire he'd seen there. "Are you sure…you don't mind sharing?" he asked.

She lifted her head again, that same proud tilt to her chin he'd seen many times before. "I'm sure."

Not wanting to give her a chance to change her mind, he quickly rid himself of his jeans and briefs, the evidence of his body's reaction to finding her lounging naked in his tub very much on display.

"Scoot forward," he said softly, wondering if the pink on her cheeks was from her heated gaze or the steamy temperature in the room.

She did as he asked, making room for him to slide in behind her. His legs traveled the length of hers until he cradled her body against his.

"Hmm, nice." Fay's words came out in a whisper as she leaned into him, resting her head against his chest.

"Your skin is so soft," he whispered, his lips at her ear as he slid his hands across her belly. "Is this okay?"

"Oh, much more than okay." She dropped her hands to the top of his bent knees and arched her back, her breasts rising from the water. "Don't stop touching me, Adam. Please don't stop."

She turned her head, her cheek brushing past his lips until moments later his mouth covered hers. Want and need exploded in his chest and he poured both into kissing her.

His hands rose to cup her breasts, loving the heaviness of them. He worked his thumbs in unison, passing back and forth over her extended nipples. Fay moaned low in her throat, her nails digging into his skin. Pressing his feet against the far end of the tub to keep himself steady, Adam matched the natural rocking motion of Fay's hips with his own, his arousal hard against the softness of her backside.

Releasing her breast, he moved one hand low over her belly until he reached the soft curls between her legs. Fay grabbed his wrist the moment his fingers stroked deep.

"Let me," he rasped against her lips.

She tightened her grip, but didn't pull his hand away. He stroked and caressed her with both hands, loving the way she whispered his name over and over again. His mouth latched onto the tender spot just beneath her ear, her excitement radiating through her body into his as it built, rising higher and higher until she cried out.

His mouth captured hers again, their kisses urgent and needy. He held tight to her as she exploded in his arms.

"Adam!" His name burst from her lips when she tore free from his kiss. "Oh, Adam!"

"I'm right here. I've got you." He loved holding her as she shuddered in her release.

"Don't... Please don't let go."

"Never," he promised with every ounce of his being. "I'm never letting go."

Fay had no idea how long they lay together in the now cool water, but she loved how he continued to touch her, trailing his fingers from her shoulders down to her wrists.

She tingled everywhere, from the inside out, as he dipped his hands beneath the water to caress her from the tops of her legs to just past her knees.

It had only taken moments for him to bring her to the same point of rapture she'd experienced in his arms almost three months ago. If she remembered correctly, he'd been as skilled back then as just now.

"Oh, boy, I think we're destined to be in here forever," she whispered, leaning back to look at his handsome face. "I don't have the strength to move one muscle."

"Well, that makes one of us." Adam angled his hips, his arousal still hard and strong against her backside.

Her face flamed, but she loved the deep chuckle that filled his chest. "Okay, maybe we should get washed up."

Adam didn't say a word when she reached for a nearby bar of soap. Instead, he sat back, laced his fingers behind his head and watched as she released the plug to let the water drain.

When she held out the soap to him, he only slowly shook his head. Unable to hold back her own smile, Fay rose to her knees before him instead and with the help of a washcloth and the handheld shower nozzle, proceeded to get the both of them very clean.

And very aroused.

Not that Adam had very far to go.

Wrapped in an oversize bath towel, she held firm to his hand when she stepped out of the tub. Adam followed and seconds later, the ground disappeared from beneath her feet when he swept her into his arms.

"Adam!" She clung to his muscular shoulders. "What are you doing?"

"Just trying to make sure you get safely to bed," he said, walking out of the bathroom. He paused to hit the light switch with his elbow on the way out; the only light in the bedroom was the small bedside lamp.

"But you're still all wet." Reaching up, she ruffled his hair, sending droplets of water raining down on his shoulders.

"Don't worry, you will be, too."

A thrill shot through her all the way to her toes at his suggestive words. "Adam…"

"Is this…" His words trailed off as he walked to the edge of his king-size bed and slowly lowered her to the blankets, stretching his naked body out beside hers. "Are we allowed to do this? I don't want to do anything to hurt you."

"You won't hurt me. Or the baby," she quickly added, her voice a hushed whisper, correctly guessing the unasked question in his eyes. It amazed her how he continued to put her—and their child—ahead of anything else.

"Stay with me, Fay." He leaned closer, pressing hot kisses along her collarbone, his hands pulling the edges of the towel free from where she'd tucked them together over her breasts. "Please, stay. I need you."

"I need you, too." She laid her hands on his jaw, loving the rough texture of his beard that had grown in during the day. "Kiss me, Adam."

He did exactly as she asked. Sweeping away the towel, he angled his mouth over hers, doing the same with his body until they were skin to skin.

She opened her legs, wanting him as close as he could be as she wrapped her arms around his back. A deep pulsing desire clawed at her, a feeling she'd never experienced before in her life. Adam left a trail of wet kisses across her breasts until he captured the hard tip of one in his mouth and sucked deeply. She arched, reaching until she gently closed her hand around his erection, marveling at the heat of his skin.

"Please, Adam…now."

He rose over her and in one slow and smooth motion joined his body with hers. She clung to him as he pressed deeper, then withdrew only to come back to her again and again. Her fingers dug into his waist, desperate to hold on as he took her higher and higher.

Cupping her head with his hand, he brought her mouth to his, their breathless pants becoming one as his mouth hovered over hers.

"With me…" he commanded, no, pleaded. "Now."

"Yes…"

Powerless to stop her heart from following her

body's demands, Fay gave into the love that had blossomed and grown inside her over the last days, weeks, every moment she'd spent with this amazing, wonderful man.

"Always, with you."

Adam shuddered and cried out her name and she was right there with him as they gave into the passion, pleasure and promise of each other.

Their chests rose and fell afterward in matching breaths until a shiver raced through Fay. Moments later, Adam had the two of them nestled beneath the covers, pulling her to his chest as he leaned against the pile of pillows.

"Hey, you're not falling asleep, are you?" he teased.

As much as she tried, Fay wasn't sure she could stay awake. "Yes, I think I'm halfway to dreamland," she said before pressing a kiss to his skin. "But I'll make you breakfast in bed come morning. How's that sound?"

"That sounds great, but…" Adam's voice trailed off as he leaned away from her. It sounded like he'd opened a drawer but Fay was too pleasantly exhausted to open her eyes and see if she was right.

"Fay?"

"Hmm?"

"Fay, open your eyes."

She tilted her head back as if she was looking at him, but still kept her eyelids closed. "Oh, do I have to?"

"Yes, you have to." He gave her a gentle squeeze with the one arm still wrapped around her. "Please."

"Oh, all right, since you said—"

The rest of her words caught in her throat as she did

what he asked only to find a velvet box literally under her nose.

"What? What are you doing?"

"Proposing." Using his thumb, Adam flipped open the hinged lid of the box one-handed. "Again."

Fay gasped.

A large solitary diamond ring sat nestled in a white satin backdrop. The stone's square shape, officially called a Princess Cut, showed off its beauty in an elegant and dramatic fashion.

"I want to make you happy, Fay. I know I can, if you only let me." Adam's tone was low, but strong. "You said we were going to be parents, and you're right about that, but we're also going to be a family. I want you to be a part of my family. I want to give you, and the baby, my name. I need you in my life."

Oh, she never expected this.

She probably should have, because of the kind of man Adam was.

She cared deeply for Adam—who was she kidding? She'd fallen in love with him—but marriage…

The first time she married she'd been too young to understand the level of commitment, the selflessness required to make a marriage work. She knew now she'd been looking for a place to belong, a family where she was wanted fully and completely. She'd foolishly thought that was what she'd found with Scott

Commitment and selflessness were part of being a parent, too. Fay knew she was ready and willing to do both—do anything for her child. But to risk her heart again?

Especially from someone who hadn't told her he

loved her? Adam had never told her what he and her father had talked about, but she knew her parents, their conservative beliefs. Was he proposing now because her father had told him to?

Fay sat up, her heart aching as she clutched the sheets to her chest. She stared at the ring, then shifted her gaze to Adam's face as he slowly lowered the box to his lap.

"You don't have to say anything. I can read your answer on your face." He snapped the lid shut and placed the box on the table next to the bed. "I thought maybe after today, after tonight, that you wanted this... wanted me. I guess I was wrong."

"I do want you, Adam."

He reached back farther and shut off the light, enveloping the room into darkness. "That's okay, I understand. Too much, too soon."

No, he was wrong.

All the words he'd just said had been wonderful, but the ones she wanted to hear most of all weren't there.

Because they weren't in his heart.

"Geez, who pissed in your Wheaties this morning?"

Adam ignored his brother and climbed into the passenger side of the helicopter, taking the headset Devlin held out to him.

He still wasn't sure how he'd gone from feeling like he was on top of the world to getting a hard kick in the ass. All in the span of just a few hours.

Saturday had been an amazing day.

A day that ended with him and Fay finally together, making love, just like he'd dreamed of for so long. He'd been so sure the moment after had been the right moment to ask her again to marry him, to create a family with him, to live and love together all the days of their lives…

"Look, I'm not going to ask for any details—"

"Good, because you wouldn't get any." Adam cut off his brother, not in the mood for Devlin's offbeat sense of humor. Not this morning. "Don't you have some pre-flight stuff you should be doing?"

"Already done. You're running a bit late." Dev's hands flew across the instrument panel. "Have a hard time getting out of bed on a Monday morning?"

Yeah, he had.

Because last night had found him once again sleeping alone.

"Sorry about ruining your Sunday. I'm sure the last thing you wanted yesterday was to spend the day on the job site," Dev said, as the helicopter lifted into the sky.

Adam braced one hand against the window, something he did every time the bird went airborne, but then he pulled in a deep breath and relaxed.

"I'm just glad those kids were okay."

Liam had called the house early yesterday morning after a group of teenagers had broken into the log home still under construction for Dean Zippenella to have a party. A few too many beers later, and an unsecured inner wall had collapsed causing three teens to be trapped.

Between the Destiny fire department, the sheriff's office and Adam's crew, they'd gotten everyone out safely, but it'd been after dark before he'd gotten home last night.

Fay had already been asleep.

In her own bed.

Adam had no idea how long he'd stood there and watched her. When he'd finally left and gone back to his own room, he found the diamond still sitting on his bedside table.

Dammit, he loved the woman and wanted her to be his wife!

Why couldn't she see that? Why had she turned him down?

For a long time, Adam watched the scenery go by below them, lost in his thoughts.

"Houston, I think we have a problem." Dev's voice came through the headset and Adam immediately picked up on the alarm in his brother's voice.

"What is it?"

"I don't know." Dev's hands deftly maneuvered over the controls. "My instrument panel is dying and we're losing power. Fast."

Outside the windows was nothing but miles and miles of dense forest. Adam was surprised to see that they'd been in the air for over thirty minutes already. "Can you get us back to Destiny?"

"I don't think so."

The helo jerked and dropped several feet. Dev cursed and tried to control the wayward machine. "If you're a praying man, I suggest you start now," he said.

"That's not funny, Dev."

"Who's laughing?" His brother glanced at him and Adam read the seriousness of their situation in his eyes.

"Send out a distress call."

"The radio's dead, too."

Adam's mind raced through the detailed emergency situations his twenty years in the military provided. "Is there a locator beacon on this craft?"

"All my electronics are shot." Dev fought to keep them level as they seesawed through the sky.

Adam reached for his cell phone. No service. He scanned the horizon looking for any open area to attempt a landing. "There's nothing but trees out there, man."

"Yeah, and we're heading straight for them. Hang on, it's going to be a bumpy landing."

Chapter Fourteen

"What do you mean they've disappeared?" Fay rose from where she'd just sat on one of the oversize leather couches in the main room of Murphy Mountain Log Homes. "People in helicopters don't just disappear."

"Dev and Adam flew out this morning for a trip to Jackson Hole." Alistair Murphy stood near the fireplace. "They planned to be gone until after dinnertime."

"I know. Adam said he wouldn't be home until late."

"Devlin should've checked in with a local airfield two hours ago," Liam added. "He hasn't and we can't reach them on the radio or their cell phones."

Fay pulled in a deep breath and looked at Elise, who was doing the same thing. She needed to stay calm, they both did. She looked at her watch. It was almost four o'clock.

"So, no one has heard from them since this morning?" she asked.

Silent nods from the rest of the Murphys were her only answers.

"So what's next?" Elise asked. "Where do we go from here?"

"Sheriff Steele is coordinating efforts with the county, search-and-rescue units and the National Park Service," Nolan said, joining the group with his cell phone to his ear. "We've still got a few hours of daylight so we're ramping up right now."

He paused and turned away, obviously listening to whomever he'd been speaking with on the other end of the line. "Right. Got it."

Nolan faced them again. "We're going to set up a command post near the east end of the Grand Tetons, about two hours from here by car on the outskirts of a town called Chapman Falls. We assume Devlin headed straight for Jackson Hole and if they had to land in the forest…"

He didn't finish his sentence. He didn't have to. All of them knew how difficult it was going to be to find two men in that amount of acreage.

"Bryant, you and Laurie coordinate things from here," Liam said. "Nolan, Ric and I are going to the command post."

"So are we," Alistair and Elise spoke in unison as Elise got to her feet, still talking. "They're our sons. We're going."

Fay stood as well. "I want to go, too."

The arguments started right away, but Fay was determined. "Look, we're wasting time. I'm going back to the house to get a few things. I'll be back here in thirty minutes."

"You boys head out and take your mother with you," Alistair said. "Fay and I will follow."

Silence filled the room for a moment before Elise leaned over and gave Fay a quick hug. Then everyone scattered. Fay waited until it was just her and Al alone in the room before she spoke.

"Please don't try to talk me out of going." She laid her hands over her belly. "I would never do anything to put my child in danger, but I have to be there. I can't lose him, Al. I just can't."

"Fay—"

"I love him." She cut off whatever Adam's father was going to say. "I am in love with your son and I was stupid not to tell him when I had the chance."

"You're going to get that chance, I'm going to make sure of it," the older man said. "But I need you to promise me you'll do your best to stay calm and if there is the slightest hint of any trouble—for you or the baby— you let me know right away."

Relief flooded her veins. "I will, I promise."

"Adam would never want you to put yourself or the baby in harm's way."

"I know that."

"You do realize I'm going to be your shadow until my son gets back here to relieve me of my sworn duties?"

Fay smiled. "You are a good man, Alistair Murphy. Adam is very lucky to be just like you."

"You make sure you tell him that once we're all back together."

Adam tugged hard on the nylon rope, making sure the tarp he'd strung between the two trees was secure.

Then he looked skyward, thankful for the warm and clear summer evening, even though he expected things to get cool overnight.

"Hey, bro. You're missing a great sunset."

He looked down at Devlin, concerned because other than a few moans when Adam had pulled his brother from the wreckage that once was their helo, Dev had fallen into unconsciousness.

Which was probably a good thing.

Adam was sure Dev had broken both his arms and his right leg in the crash. They'd come down hard, but he credited Devlin for the fact that both of them were still alive. The helo had broken into pieces, but thankfully the survival kit stowed beneath the rear seats had landed not too far from them.

They had fire-starting materials, two sleeping bags, a signal mirror, nylon cording and a weatherproof tarp that Adam had just used to create shelter for them for tonight.

He checked his watch. It'd been almost nine hours since they'd taken off. Someone must have noticed by now they were missing and if he knew his family, a search and rescue was already underway.

His training told him the best thing to do was to stay as close to the wreckage as possible and keep his brother comfortable, no small feat seeing how he had to splint both of Dev's arms and his leg in hopes of keeping them stable before wrapping him in one of the sleeping bags to keep him warm.

"Don't worry, Dev. We've got enough water for a few days and some trail mix and granola bars. We're going to make it through this." Adam knelt at his brother's side, worried when his forehead felt warm to the touch. Suddenly, Dev moaned and started moving his head.

"Hey, take it easy. You're fine. We both are." His brother opened his eyes and Adam read confusion and pain there. "Hey, bro. You with me? Can you hear me?"

Devlin groaned. "Damn, I hurt."

"Well, don't move. I mean it," he said, putting his hand back to his brother's forehead. "You're busted up pretty good."

"Where?"

Adam told him about his suspected injuries and Devlin closed his eyes.

"Just some scratches and bruises." And thankfully no signs of post-traumatic stress. "Hey, I've found some ibuprofen here. Think you can get a couple down? It's all we've got."

His brother nodded, and was able to swallow a couple of the pills and a tiny bit of water. He then drifted off to sleep, leaving Adam alone to build a fire.

And think.

About Fay, about the baby and how he had to get back to them.

No more pressure, no more proposals. All he wanted was to spend the rest of his life with Fay and if she needed more time before she was ready to take things between them any further, then he'd give her all the time she needed.

That's what people in love did. What was best for the other person, even if it wasn't what they wanted for themselves.

He loved her.

It was as simple as that and if Fay needed—

Staring into the fire, Adam rewound everything he'd said to Fay on Saturday night. Did he really say all those things to her and not once tell her that he loved her?

"Get us home." Adam offered up a fervent prayer to whoever might be listening. "Get us safely home and I promise that Fay will never again doubt how much I love her and how important she and the baby are to me."

Fay had agreed that if Adam and Devlin weren't found after forty-eight hours, she'd return to Destiny. It'd been an easy promise to make as she'd been so sure...

"Both of my sons are strong men." Alastair leaned into the window of his wife's car. "Adam didn't spend twenty years in the Air Force without learning a thing or two about survival. They are going to be found. Soon."

Fay nodded as she secured the seat belt over her hips. The command post for the search and rescue resembled a small tent city, but she and Elise had taken a room at a small motel in nearby Chapman Falls.

Not that she'd gotten much sleep in the cramped quarters over the last two nights, and she was feeling the effects. She needed to take care of their child and that meant returning home.

"You'll call me every hour with an update?" She held tight to Alastair's hand. "Promise?"

"I promise, but I'm going to call Elise because you're supposed to head straight to bed," Al said.

Fay nodded. The family had enough to worry about

here as the search for Adam and Devlin continued, they didn't need to add her to their list. "I promise. Straight to bed after a house call from my doctor."

She had called Liz on the way to the command post and they'd spoken often over the last few days. Fay had heard the relief in her friend's voice each time she assured her she was feeling fine, but was glad when Liz had said she'd stop by and check on her once Fay got back to town.

"Okay, let's go."

By nightfall, Fay was back home and trying to rest as she waited for word. Both she and the baby were fine, although Liz had an emergency delivery and had to head back to Laramie.

Fay wanted to be back in her bed, and knew Elise felt the same way. She promised she would be fine and would call if there were any issues.

Everyone in town knew about the search for Adam and Devlin, with many of the same men who'd been here just last weekend to work on the barn volunteering to take part.

"He's going to come home to us," Fay said as she stroked Shadow's soft fur. "To all of us."

The dog had been overjoyed to see her after spending a couple of days with Nolan's children, but Fay could tell the animal missed Adam. The two of them crawled beneath the covers on his king-size bed and she checked in with Elise.

Still no word.

Rolling to her side, Fay spotted the velvet box still sitting on the bedside table. She reached for it, cradling it in her palm for a long moment before she opened it.

The beauty of the ring took her breath away. Again. She couldn't believe Adam had gotten such an amazing gift for her. Lifting it gently from the satin tufting, she held it up, marveling at how it sparkled in the light. She then slowly slid it onto the third finger of her left hand. A little loose, but it would fit perfectly by the time she was ready to give birth next year.

Lying back against the pillows, she stared at the ring until her eyes grew heavy. She couldn't wait to show Adam how much she wanted to wear his ring, how she wanted another chance to answer his question. There were issues they needed to deal with, specifically financial assistance for Mavis, but they would find a way. If they just got the chance…

"I knew that ring was meant for you the moment I saw it."

Fay gasped, her eyes flying open at the sound of Adam's voice, and there he was, sitting right next to her on the bed. She flew into his arms, tears welling in her eyes the moment she felt his strong embrace.

"Oh! You're home! You're safe!" She pressed her hands to his shoulders, his back, testing to see if he was really real. "I'm not dreaming. Please tell me I'm not dreaming!"

"Shh, sweetheart, yes, it's me."

Adam held her close, but she pulled back. She had to see his face, to touch, to make sure. Fay trailed her fingers through his hair and over his jaw, staring into the dark brown eyes she'd come to love in just a few weeks.

It was then she realized bright sunlight streamed through the windows.

"What time is it? When did you get here?" The questions fell from her lips. "How did they find you? Is Dev with you? Are you both okay?"

Adam grinned. "It's Thursday afternoon, just now, skilled searchers who knew what they were doing and yes, other than needing a long, hot shower and some food, I'm just fine."

Fay quickly processed his answers, realized he'd left out the one about his brother. "Devlin? Please tell me he's okay."

The smile faded from Adam's face. "He was banged up pretty bad in the crash. They med-flighted him straight to the hospital in Cheyenne. He broke both his arms and his leg. They needed to get him into surgery right away."

"Oh, Adam!"

"The EMTs who checked him out said they thought he'll be fine…over time. Dev's young and he's got that stubborn Irish steak in him." His smile returned. "Runs in the family, I think."

"If that's true, I think I'm a Murphy, too."

"There's nothing I want more than for you to have my name, to be my wife." Adam's tone grew serious as he drew her hands away from his neck, holding them tightly in his own. "All I could think about while I was stuck out in the wilderness was how stupid I was to push you, how you needed to find your own way to whatever it is we're building here. You need time, Fay, and I'm willing to give you all the time in the world."

"Adam, I—"

"I love you." He rushed over her words. "I think I have, in my own way, for a long time. These last few weeks…my feelings for you, for the baby, have only grown stronger and more certain. My only mistake was not telling you exactly how I felt the moment I realized what it was, but now that I do I plan to tell you often—"

"Wait!" Fay laughed and pulled one hand free, gently laying it across his lips, stopping his speech. "I love you, too, and I don't need any more time to know the most important thing to me is you, us and this baby. I want to be your wife, I want us to be a family."

She gently brushed her fingers over his bottom lip, loving how his eyes darkened at her touch. "So, if you'll do me the honor of becoming my husband…"

"Are you asking me to marry you?"

Fay smiled. "Yes, I'm asking you to marry me."

Placing one hand gently over her belly, Adam reached for her left hand, his thumb brushing across the ring. "My answer is yes. Just in case you were wondering, it's definitely yes!"

* * * * *

THE ANNIVERSARY PARTY

Dear Reader,

I am a big believer in celebrating milestones, and for Special Edition, this is a big one! Thirty years… it hardly seems possible, and yet April 1982 was indeed, yep, thirty years ago! When I walked into the Harlequin offices (only *twenty* years ago, but still), the first books I worked on were Special Edition. I loved the line instantly—for its breadth and its depth, and for its fabulous array of authors, some of whom I've been privileged to work with for twenty years, and some of whom are newer, but no less treasured, friends.

When it came time to plan our thirtieth anniversary celebration, we wanted to give our readers something from the heart—not to mention something from our very beloved April 2012 lineup. So many thanks to RaeAnne Thayne, Christine Rimmer, Susan Crosby, Christyne Butler, Gina Wilkins and Cindy Kirk for their contributions to *The Anniversary Party*. The Morgans, Diana and Frank, are celebrating their thirtieth anniversary along with us. Like us, they've had a great thirty years, and they're looking forward to many more. Like us, though there may be some obstacles along the way, they're getting their happily ever after.

Which is what we wish you, Dear Reader. Thanks for coming along for the first thirty years of Special Edition—we hope you'll be with us for many more!

We hope you enjoy *The Anniversary Party*.

Here's to the next thirty!

All the best,

Gail Chasan
Senior Editor, Special Edition

Chapter One
by RaeAnne Thayne

With the basket of crusty bread sticks she had baked that afternoon in one arm and a mixed salad—*insalata mista,* as the Italians would say—in the other, Melissa Morgan walked into her sister's house and her jaw dropped.

"Oh, my word, Ab! This looks incredible! When did you start decorating? A month ago?"

Predictably, Abby looked a little wild-eyed. Her sister was one of those type A personalities who always sought perfection, whether that was excelling in her college studies, where she'd emerged with a summa cum laude, or decorating for their parents' surprise thirtieth anniversary celebration.

Abby didn't answer for a moment. She was busy arranging a plant in the basket of a rusty bicycle resting against one wall so the greenery spilled over the top, almost to the front tire. Melissa had no idea how she'd managed it but somehow Abby had hung wooden lattice from her ceiling to form a faux pergola over her dining table. Grapevines, fairy lights and more greenery had been woven through the lattice and, at various intervals, candles hung in colored jars like something out of a Tuscan vineyard.

Adorning the walls were framed posters of Venice and the beautiful and calming Lake Como.

"It feels like a month," Abby finally answered, "but actually, I only started last week. Greg helped me hang the lattice. I couldn't have done it without him."

The affection in her sister's voice caused a funny little twinge inside Melissa. Abby and her husband had one of those perfect relationships. They clearly adored each other, no matter what.

She wished she could say the same thing about Josh. After a year of dating, shouldn't she have a little more confidence in their relationship? If someone had asked her a month ago if she thought her boyfriend loved her, she would have been able to answer with complete assurance in the affirmative, but for the past few weeks something had changed. He'd been acting so oddly—dodging phone calls, canceling plans, avoiding her questions.

He seemed to be slipping away more every day. As melodramatic as it sounded, she didn't know how she would survive if he decided to break things off.

Breathe, she reminded herself. She didn't want to ruin the anniversary dinner by worrying about Josh. For now, she really needed to focus on her wonderful parents and how very much they deserved this celebration she and Abby had been planning for a long time.

"You and Greg have really outdone yourself. I love all the little details. The old wine bottles, the flowers. Just beautiful. I know Mom and Dad will be thrilled with your hard work." She paused. "I can only see one little problem."

Abby looked vaguely panicked. "What? What's missing?"

Melissa shook her head ruefully. "Nothing. That's the problem. I was supposed to be helping you. That's why I'm here early, right? Have you left anything for me to do?"

"Are you kidding? I've still got a million things to do. The chicken cacciatore is just about ready to go into the oven. Why don't you help me set the table?"

"Sure," she said, following her sister into the kitchen.

"You talked to Louise, right?" Abby asked.

"Yes. She had everything ready when I stopped at her office on my way over here. I've got a huge gift basket in the car. You should see it. She really went all out. Biscotti, gourmet cappuccino mix, even a bottle of prosecco."

"What about the tickets and the itinerary?" Abby had that panicked look again.

"Relax, Abs. It's all there. She's been amazing. I think she just might be as scarily organized as you are."

Abby made a face. "Did you have a chance to go over the details?"

"She printed everything out and included a copy for us, as well as Mom and Dad. In addition to the plane tickets and the hotel information and the other goodies, she sent over pamphlets, maps, even an Italian-English dictionary and a couple of guidebooks."

"Perfect! They're going to be so surprised."

"Surprised and happy, I hope," Melissa answered, loading her arms with the deep red chargers and honey-gold plates her sister indicated, which perfectly matched the theme for the evening.

"How could they be anything else? They finally have the chance to enjoy the perfect honeymoon they missed out on the first time." Abby smiled, looking more than a little starry-eyed. Despite being married for several years, her sister was a true romantic.

"This has to be better than the original," she said. "The bar was set pretty low thirty years ago, judging by all the stories they've told us over the years. Missed trains, lousy hotels, disappearing luggage."

"Don't forget the pickpocket that stole their cash and passports."

Melissa had to smile. Though their parents' stories always made their honeymoon thirty years ago sound dismal, Frank and Diane always laughed when they shared them, as if they had viewed the whole thing as a huge adventure.

She wanted that. She wanted to share that kind of joy and laughter and tears with Josh. The adventure that was life.

Her smile faded, replaced by that ache of sadness that always seemed so close these days. *Oh, Josh.* She reached into the silverware drawer, avoiding her sister's gaze.

"Okay. What's wrong?" Abby asked anyway.

She forced a smile. "Nothing. I'm just a little tired, that's all."

"Late night with Josh?" her sister teased.

Before she could stop them, tears welled up and spilled over. She blinked them back but not before her sharp-eyed sister caught them.

"What did I say?" Abby asked with a stunned look.

"Nothing. I just…I didn't have a late night with Josh. Not last night, not last week, not for the last two weeks. He's avoiding my calls and canceled our last two dates. Even when we're together, it's like he's not there. I know he's busy at work but…I think he's planning to break up with me."

Abby's jaw sagged and Melissa saw shock and something else, something furtive, shift across Abby's expression.

"That can't be true. It just…can't be."

She wanted to believe that, too. "I'm sorry. I shouldn't have said anything. Forget it. You've worked so hard to make this night perfect and I don't want to ruin it."

Abby shook her head. "You need to put that wacky idea out of your head right now. Josh is crazy about you. It's clear to anybody who has ever seen the two of you together for five seconds. He couldn't possibly be thinking of breaking things off."

"I'm sure you're right," she lied. Too much evidence pointed otherwise. Worst of all was the casual kiss good-night the past few times she'd seen him, instead of one of their deep, emotional, soul-sharing kisses that made her toes curl.

"I'm serious, Missy. Trust me on this. I'm absolutely

positive he's not planning to break up with you. Not Josh. He loves you. In fact…"

She stopped, biting her lip, and furiously turned back to the chicken.

"In fact what?"

Abby's features were evasive. "In fact, would he be out right now with Greg buying the wine and champagne for tonight if he didn't want to have anything to do with the Morgan family?"

Out of the corner of her gaze, Melissa saw that amazingly decorated dining room again, the magical setting her sister had worked so hard to create for their parents who loved each other dearly. She refused to ruin this night for Abby and the rest of her family. For now, she would focus on the celebration and forget the tiny cracks in her heart.

She pasted on a smile and grabbed the napkins, with their rings formed out of entwined grapevine hearts. "You're right. I'm being silly. I'm sure everything will be just fine. Anyway, tonight is for Mom and Dad. That's the important thing."

Abby gave her a searching look and Melissa couldn't help thinking that even with the worry lines on her forehead, Abby seemed to glow tonight.

"It is about them, isn't it?" Abby murmured. Though Melissa's arms were full, her sister reached around the plates and cutlery to give her a hug. "Trust me, baby sister. Everything will be just fine."

Melissa dearly wanted to believe her and as she returned to the dining room, she did her very best to ignore the ache of fear that something infinitely dear was slipping away.

* * *

"Hello? Are you still in there?"

His friend Greg's words jerked Josh out of his daze and he glanced up. "Yeah. Sorry. Did you say something?"

"Only about three times. I've been asking your opinion about the champagne and all I'm getting in return is a blank stare. You're a million miles away, man, which is not really helping out much here."

This just might be the most important day of his life. Who could blame a guy if he couldn't seem to string two thoughts together?

"Sorry. I've got a lot of things on my mind."

"And champagne is obviously not one of those things."

He made a face. "It rarely is. I'm afraid I'm more of a Sam Adams kind of guy."

"I hear you. Why do you think I asked you to come along and help me pick out the wine and champagne for tonight?"

He had wondered that himself. "Because my car has a bigger trunk?"

Greg laughed, which eased Josh's nerves a little. He had to admit, he had liked the guy since he met him a year ago when he first started dating Melissa. Josh was married to Melissa's sister, Abby, and if things worked out the way he hoped, they would be brothers-in-law in the not-so-distant future.

"It's only the six of us for dinner," Greg reminded him. "I'm not exactly buying cases here. So what do you think?"

He turned back to the racks of bottles. "No idea. Which one is more expensive?"

Greg picked one up with a fancy label that certainly looked pricey.

"Excellent choice." The snooty clerk who had mostly been ignoring them since they walked in finally deigned to approach them.

"You think so?" Greg asked. "We're celebrating a big occasion."

"You won't be disappointed, I assure you. What else can I help you find?"

Sometime later—and with considerably lightened wallets—the two of them carried two magnums of champagne and two bottles of wine out to Josh's car.

"I, uh, need to make one last quick stop," he said after pulling into traffic. "Do you mind waiting?"

"No problem. The party doesn't start for another two hours. We've got plenty of time."

When Josh pulled up in front of an assuming storefront a few moments later, Greg looked at the sign above the door then back at him with eyebrows raised. "Wow. Seriously? Tonight? I thought Abby was jumping the gun when she said she suspected you were close to proposing. She's always right, that beautiful wife of mine. Don't tell her I said that."

Josh shifted, uncomfortably aware his fingers were shaking a little as he undid his seatbelt. "I bought the ring two weeks ago. When the jeweler told me it would be ready today, I figured that was a sign."

"You're a brave man to pick a ring out without her."

Panic clutched at his gut again, but he took a deep breath and pushed it away. He wanted to make his proposal perfect. Part of that, to his mind, was the element of surprise.

"I found a bridal magazine at Melissa's apartment kind of hidden under a stack of books and she had the page folded down on this ring. I snapped a quick picture with my phone and took that in to the jeweler."

"Nice." Greg's admiring look settled his stomach a little.

"I figure, if she doesn't like it, we can always reset the stone, right?"

"So when are you going to pop the question?"

"I haven't figured that out yet. I thought maybe when I take her home after the party tonight, we might drive up to that overlook above town."

"That could work."

"What about you? How did you propose to Abby?"

"Nothing very original, I'm afraid. I took her to dinner at La Maison Marie. She loves that place. Personally, I think you're only paying for overpriced sauce, but what can do? Anyway, after dinner, she kept acting like she was expecting something. I *did* take her along to shop for rings a few weeks earlier but hadn't said anything to her since. She seemed kind of disappointed when the dessert came and no big proposal. So we were walking around on the grounds after dinner and we walked past this waterfall and pond she liked. I pretended I tripped over something and did a stupid little magician sleight of hand and pulled out the ring box."

"Did you do the whole drop-to-your-knee thing?"

"Yeah. It seemed important to Abby. Women remember that kind of thing."

"I hope I don't forget that part."

"Don't sweat it. When the moment comes, whatever you do will be right for the two of you, I promise."

"I hope so."

The depth of his love for Melissa still took him by surprise. He loved her with everything inside him and wanted to give her all the hearts and flowers and romance she could ever want.

"It will be," Greg said. "Anyway, look at how lousy Frank and Diane's marriage started out. Their honeymoon sounded like a nightmare but thirty years later they can still laugh about it."

That was what he wanted with Melissa. Thirty years—and more—of laughter and joy and love.

He just had to get through the proposal first.

Chapter Two
by Christine Rimmer

"Frank. The light is yellow. Frank!" Diana Morgan stomped the passenger-side floor of the Buick. Hard. If only she had the brakes on her side.

Frank Morgan pulled to a smooth stop as the light went red. "There," he said, in that calm, deep, untroubled voice she'd always loved. "We're stopped. No need to wear a hole in the floor."

Diana glanced over at her husband of thirty years. She loved him so much. There were a whole lot of things to worry about in life, but Frank's love was the one thing Diana never doubted. He belonged to her, absolutely, as she belonged to him, and he'd given her two beautiful, perfect daughters. Abby and Melissa were all grown up now.

The years went by way too fast.

Diana sent her husband another glance. Thirty years

together. Amazing. She still loved just looking at him. He was the handsomest man she'd ever met, even at fifty-seven. Nature had been kind to him. He had all his hair and it was only lightly speckled with gray. She smoothed her own shoulder-length bob. No gray there, either. Her hair was still the same auburn shade it had been when she married him. Only in her case, nature didn't have a thing to do with it.

A man only grew more distinguished over the years. A woman had to work at it.

The light turned green. Frank hit the gas.

Too hard, Diana thought. But she didn't say a word. She only straightened her teal-blue silk blouse, re-crossed her legs and tried not to make impatient, wor-ried noises. Frank was a wonderful man. But he drove too fast.

Abby and her husband, Greg, were having them over for dinner tonight. They were on their way there now—to Abby's house. Diana was looking forward to the evening. But she was also dreading it. Something was going on with Abby. A mother knows these things.

And something was bothering Melissa, too. Diana's younger daughter was still single. She'd been going out with Josh Wright for a year now. It was a serious rela-tionship.

But was there something wrong between Josh and Melissa? Diana had a sense about these things, a sort of radar for emotional disturbances, especially when it came to her daughters. Right now, tonight, Diana had a suspicion that something wasn't right—both between Melissa and Josh *and* between Abby and Greg.

"Remember Venice?" Frank gave her a fond glance.

She smiled at him—and then stiffened. "Frank. Eyes on the road."

"All right, all right." He patiently faced front again. "Remember that wonderful old hotel on the Grand Canal?"

She made a humphing sound. "It was like the rest of our honeymoon. Nothing went right."

"I loved every moment of it," he said softly.

She reminded him, "You know what happened at that hotel in Venice, how they managed to lose our luggage somewhere between the front desk and our room. How hard can it be, to get the suitcases to the right room? And it smelled a bit moldy in the bathroom, didn't you think?"

"All I remember is you, Diana. Naked in the morning light." He said it softly. Intimately.

She shivered a little, drew in a shaky breath and confessed, "Oh, yes. That. I remember that, too." It was one of the best things about a good marriage. The shared memories. Frank had seen her naked in Venice when they were both young. Together, they had heard Abby's first laugh, watched Melissa as she learned to walk, staggering and falling, but then gamely picking herself right back up and trying again. Together, they had made it through all those years that drew them closer, through the rough times as well as the happy ones....

A good marriage.

Until very recently, she'd been so sure that Abby and Greg were happy. But were they? Really? And what about Melissa and Josh?

Oh, Lord. Being a mother was the hardest job in the world. They grew up. But they stayed in your heart.

And when they were suffering, you ached right along with them.

"All right," Frank said suddenly in an exasperated tone. "You'd better just tell me, Diana. You'd better just say it, whatever it is."

Diana sighed. Deeply. "Oh, Frank…"

"Come on," he coaxed, pulling to another stop at yet another stoplight—at the very last possible second. She didn't even stomp the floor that time, she was that upset. "Tell me," he insisted.

Tears pooled in her eyes and clogged her throat. She sniffed them back. "I wasn't going to do it. I wasn't going to interfere. I wasn't even going to say a word…"

He flipped open the armrest and whipped out a tissue. "Dry your eyes."

"Oh, Frank…" She took the tissue and dabbed at her lower lid. If she wasn't careful, her makeup would be a total mess.

"Now," Frank said, reaching across to pat her knee. "Tell me about it. Whatever it is, you know you'll feel better once we've talked it over."

The light changed. "Go," she said on a sob.

He drove on. "I'm waiting."

She sniffed again. "I think something's wrong between Abby and Greg. And not only that, there's something going on with Melissa, too. I think Melissa's got…a secret, you know? A secret that is worrying her terribly."

"Why do you think something's going on between Abby and Greg?"

"I sensed it. You know how sensitive I am— Oh,

God. Do you think Abby and Greg are breaking up? Do you think he might be seeing someone else?"

"Whoa. Diana. Slow down."

"Well, I am *worried.* I am *so* worried. And Melissa. She is suffering. I can hear it in her voice when I talk to her."

"But you haven't told me *why* you think there might be something wrong—with Melissa, or between Abby and Greg. Did Abby say something to you?"

"Of course not. She wants to protect me."

"What about Melissa?"

"What do you *mean,* what about Melissa?"

"Well, did you *ask* her if something is bothering her?"

Another sob caught in Diana's throat. She swallowed it. "I couldn't. I didn't want to butt in."

Frank eased the car to the shoulder and stopped. "Diana," he said. That was all. Just her name.

It was more than enough. "Don't you look at me like that, Frank Morgan."

"Diana, I hate to say this—"

"Then don't. Just don't. And why are we stopped? We'll be late. Even with family, you know I always like to be on time."

"Diana…"

She waved her soggy tissue at him. "Drive, Frank. Just drive."

He leaned closer across the console. "Sweetheart…"

She sagged in her seat. "Oh, fine. What?"

"You know what you're doing, don't you?" He said it gently. But still. She knew exactly what he was getting at and she didn't like it one bit.

She sighed and dropped the wadded tissue in the little wastepaper bag she always carried in the car. "Well, I know you're bound to tell me, now don't I?"

He took her hand, kissed the back of it.

"Don't try to butter me up," she muttered.

"You're jumping to conclusions again," he said tenderly.

"Am not."

"Yes, you are. You've got nothin'. Zip. Admit it. No solid reason why you think Melissa has a secret or why you think Abby and Greg are suddenly on the rocks."

"I don't need a solid reason. I can *feel* it." She laid her hand over her heart. "Here."

"You know it's very possible that what's really going on is a surprise anniversary party for us, don't you?"

Diana smoothed her hair. "What? You mean tonight?"

"That's right. Tonight."

"Oh, I suppose. It could be." She pictured their dear faces. She loved them so much. "They are the sweetest girls, aren't they?"

"The best. I'm the luckiest dad in the world—not to mention the happiest husband."

Diana leaned toward him and kissed him. "You *are* a very special man." She sank back against her seat— and remembered how worried she was. "But Frank, if this *is* a party, it's still not *it*."

"It?" He looked bewildered. Men could be so thick-headed sometimes.

Patiently, she reminded him, "The awful, secret things that are going on with our daughters."

He bent in close, kissed her cheek and then brushed

his lips across her own. "We are going to dinner at our daughter's house," he whispered. "We are going to have a wonderful time. You are not going to snoop around trying to find out if something's wrong with Abby. You're not going to worry about Melissa."

"I hate you, Frank."

"No, you don't. You love me *almost* as much as I love you."

She wrinkled her nose at him. "More. I love you more."

He kissed her again. "Promise you won't snoop and you'll stop jumping to conclusions?"

"And if I don't, what? We'll sit here on the side of the road all night?"

"Promise."

"Fine. All right. I promise."

He touched her cheek, a lovely, cherishing touch. "Can we go to Abby's now?"

"I'm not the one who stopped the car."

He only looked at her reproachfully.

She couldn't hold out against him. She never could. "Oh, all right. I've promised, already, okay? Now, let's go."

With a wry smile, he retreated back behind the wheel and eased the car forward into the flow of traffic again.

Abby opened the door. "Surprise!" Abby, Greg, Melissa and Josh all shouted at once. They all started clapping.

Greg announced, "Happy Anniversary!" The rest of them chimed in with "Congratulations!" and "Thirty years!" and "Wahoo!"

Frank was laughing. "Well, what do you know?"

Diana said nothing. One look in her older daughter's big brown eyes and she knew for certain that she wasn't just imagining things. Something was going on in Abby's life. Something important.

They all filed into the dining room, where the walls were decorated with posters of the Grand Canal and the Tuscan countryside, of the Coliseum and the small, beautiful town of Bellagio on Lake Como. The table was set with Abby's best china and tall candles gave a golden glow.

Greg said, "We thought, you know, an Italian theme—in honor of your honeymoon."

"It's lovely," said Diana, going through the motions, hugging first Greg and then Josh.

"Thank you," said Frank as he clapped his son-in-law on the back and shook hands with Josh.

Melissa came close. "Mom." She put on a smile. But her eyes were as shadowed as Abby's. "Happy thirtieth anniversary."

Diana grabbed her and hugged her. No doubt about it. Melissa looked miserable, too.

Yes, Diana had promised Frank that she would mind her own business.

But, well, sometimes a woman just couldn't keep that kind of promise. Sometimes a woman had to find a way to get to the bottom of a bad situation for the sake of the ones she loved most of all.

By the end of the evening, no matter what, Diana would find out the secrets her daughters were keeping from her.

Frank leaned close. "Don't even think about it."

She gave him her sweetest smile. "Happy anniversary, darling."

Chapter Three
by Susan Crosby

Abby Morgan DeSena and her husband, Greg, had hosted quite a few dinner parties during their three years of marriage, but none as special as this one—a celebration of Abby's parents' thirtieth wedding anniversary. Abby and her younger sister, Melissa, had spent weeks planning the Italian-themed party as a sweet reminder for their parents of their honeymoon, and now that the main meal was over, Abby could say, well, so far, so good.

For someone who planned everything down to the last detail, that was high praise. They were on schedule. First, antipasti and wine in the living room, then chicken cacciatore, crusty bread sticks and green salad in the dining room.

But for all that the timetable had been met and the food praised and devoured, an air of tension hovered over the six people at the table, especially between Melissa and her boyfriend, Josh, who were both acting out of character.

"We had chicken cacciatore our first night in Bellagio, remember, Diana?" Abby's father said to her mother as everyone sat back, sated. "And lemon sorbet in prosecco."

"The waiter knocked my glass into my lap," Diana reminded him.

"Your napkin caught most of it, and he fixed you another one. He even took it off the tab. On our new-lywed budget, it made a difference." He brought his wife's hand to his lips, his eyes twinkling. "And it was delicious, wasn't it? Tart and sweet and bubbly."

Diana blushed, making Abby wonder if the memory involved more than food. It was inspiring seeing her parents so openly in love after thirty years.

Under the table, Abby felt her hand being squeezed and looked at her own beloved husband. Greg winked, as if reading her mind.

"Well, we don't have sorbet and prosecco," Abby said, standing and stacking dinner plates. "But we certainly have dessert. Please sit down, Mom. You're our guest. Melissa and I will take care of everything."

It didn't take long to clear the table.

"Mom and Dad loved the dinner, didn't they?" Melissa asked as they entered Abby's contemporary kitchen.

"They seemed to," Abby answered, although unsure whether she believed her own words. Had her parents noticed the same tension Abby had? Her mother's gaze had flitted from Melissa to Josh to Abby to Greg all evening, as if searching for clues. It'd made Abby more nervous with every passing minute, and on a night she'd been looking forward to, a night of sweet surprises.

"How about you? Did you enjoy the meal?" Abby asked Melissa, setting dishes in the sink, then started the coffeemaker brewing. "You hardly touched your food."

She shrugged. "I guess I snacked on too many bread sticks before dinner."

Abby took out a raspberry tiramisu from the refrigerator while studying her sister, noting how stiffly Melissa held herself, how shaky her hands were as she rinsed the dinner plates. She seemed fragile. It wasn't a word Abby usually applied to her sister. The conversation they'd had earlier in the evening obviously hadn't set Melissa's mind at ease, but Abby didn't know what else to say to her tightly wrung sister. Only time—and Josh—could relieve Melissa's anxiety.

Abby set the fancy dessert on the counter next to six etched-crystal parfait glasses.

Melissa approached, drying her hands, then picked up one of the glasses. "Grandma gave these to you, didn't she?"

"Mmm-hmm. Three years ago as a wedding present. I know it's a cliché, but it seems like yesterday." Abby smiled at her sister, remembering the wedding, revisiting her wonderful marriage. She couldn't ask for a better husband, friend and partner than Greg. "Grandma plans to give you the other six glasses at your wedding. When we both have big family dinners, we can share them. It'll be our tradition."

Melissa's face paled. Her eyes welled. Horrified, Abby dropped the spoon and reached for her.

"I—I'll grab the gift basket from your office," Melissa said, taking a couple steps back then rushing out.

Frustrated, Abby pressed her face into her hands. If she were the screaming type, she would've screamed. If she were a throw-the-pots-around type, she would've done that, too, as noisily as possible. It would've felt *good*.

"I thought Melissa was in here with you," said a male voice from behind her.

Abby spun around and glared at Josh Wright, the source of Melissa's problems—and subsequently Abby's—as he peeked into the kitchen. He could be the solution, too, if only he'd act instead of sitting on his hands.

"She's getting the anniversary gift from my office," Abby said through gritted teeth, digging deep for the composure she'd inherited from her father.

Josh came all the way into the room. He looked as strained as Melissa. "Need some help?" he asked, shoving his hands into his pockets instead of going in search of Melissa.

"Coward." Abby began dishing up six portions of tiramisu.

"Guilty," Josh said, coming up beside her. "Give me a job. I can't sit still."

"You can pour the decaf into that carafe next to the coffeemaker."

Full of nervous energy, his hands shaking as much as Melissa's had earlier, he got right to the task, fumbling at every step, slopping coffee onto the counter.

"Relax, would you, Josh?" Abby said, exasperated. "You're making everyone jumpy, but especially Melissa. My sister is her mother's daughter, you know. They both have a flair for the dramatic, but this time Melissa is honestly thrown by your behavior. She's on the edge, and it's not of her own making."

"But it'll all come out okay in the end?"

The way he turned the sentence into a question had Abby staring at him. He and her kid sister were a study in contrasts, Melissa with her black hair and green eyes, Josh all blond and blue-eyed. They'd been dating for a year, were head over heels in love with each other, seeming to validate the theory that opposites attract. It was rare that they weren't touching or staring into each other's eyes, communicating silently.

Tonight was different, however, and Abby knew why. She just didn't know if they would all survive the suspense.

"Whether or not it all turns out okay in the end depends on how long you take to pop the question," Abby said, dropping her voice to a whisper.

"You know I'm planning the perfect proposal," he whispered back. "Your husband gave me advice, but if you'd like to add yours, I'm listening."

She couldn't tell him that Melissa thought he was about to break up with her—that was hers to say. But Abby could offer some perspective.

"Here's my advice, Josh, and it has nothing to do with how to set a romantic scene that she'll remember the rest of her life. My advice is simple—do it sooner rather than later." She spoke in a normal tone again, figuring even if someone came into the room, they wouldn't suspect what she and Josh were talking about. "When Greg and I were in college, I misunderstood something he said. Instead of asking him to clarify it, I stewed. And stewed some more. I blew it all out of proportion."

She dug deep into memories she'd long ago put aside. "Here's what happens to a couple at times like that. He asks what's wrong, and she says it's nothing. He asks again. She *insists* it's nothing. A gulf widens that can't be crossed because there's no longer a bridge between them, one you used to travel easily. It doesn't even matter how much love you share. Once trust is gone, once the ability to talk to each other openly and freely goes away, the relationship begins to unravel. Sometimes it takes weeks, sometimes months, even years, but it happens and there's no fixing it."

"But you fixed it."

They almost hadn't, Abby remembered. They came so close to breaking up. "At times like that, it can go either way. Even strong partners struggle sometimes in a marriage."

"How do you get through those times?"

"You put on a smile for everyone, then you try to work it out alone together so that no one else gets involved."

"Don't you talk to your mom? She's had a long, successful marriage. She'd give good advice, wouldn't she?"

Abby smiled as she pictured her sweet, sometimes overwrought mother. "Mom's the last one I'd ask for advice," she said.

* * *

"I'm going to see what's taking so long," Diana said to her husband, laying her napkin on the table.

"Diana." Implied in his tone of voice were the words he didn't speak aloud—*Don't borrow trouble.*

"I'm sure they'll be right out," Greg said, standing, suddenly looking frantic. Her cool, calm son-in-law never panicked.

It upped her determination to see what was wrong. Because something definitely was.

"I'm going." Diana headed toward the kitchen. She could hear Abby speaking quietly.

"I adore my mother, but she makes mountains out of molehills. Greg and I are a team. We keep our problems to ourselves. And you know she would take my side, as any parent would, and that isn't fair to Greg. She might hold on to her partiality long after I've forgotten the argument. So you see, Josh, sometimes the best way to handle personal problems is to keep other people in the dark. Got it?"

"Clear as a bell."

Diana slapped a hand over her mouth and slid a few feet along the wall outside the kitchen before she let out an audible gasp. Her first born *was* keeping her in the dark about something, just as Diana had suspected. And Frank had pooh-poohed the whole thing.

Men just didn't get it. It wasn't called women's intuition for nothing—and she wasn't just a woman but a mother. Mothers saw every emotion on their children's faces, knew every body movement.

She'd *known* something was wrong with Abby. Now it'd been verified, not by rumor but by the person in question, no less. Abby and Greg were on the verge of separating. Her daughter had hidden their problems, not seeking advice from the one who loved her most in the world. Diana could've helped, too, she was sure of it.

Keep other people in the dark. The words stung. She wasn't "other people." She was Abby's mother.

And what about Melissa? What was her problem— because she definitely had one, something big, too. Had she confided in Abby?

Diana moved out of range, not wanting to hear more distressing words, not on the anniversary of the most wonderful day of her life. But she had to tell Frank what she'd learned, had to share the awful news with her own partner so that she could make it through the rest of the evening.

At least she could count on Frank to understand.

She hoped.

Chapter Four
by Christyne Butler

Don't think, don't feel.

Just keep breathing and you'll get through this night unscathed.

Unscathed, but with a broken heart.

Melissa squared her shoulders, brushed the wetness from her cheeks and heaved a shuddering breath that shook her all the way to her toes.

There. Don't you feel calmer?

No, she didn't, but that wasn't anyone's fault but her own.

She'd fallen in love with Josh on their very first date and after tonight, she'd probably never see him again.

The past two weeks had been crazy at her job. Trying to make it through what had been ten hours without her usual caffeine fix, having decided that two cups of coffee and three diet sodas a day weren't the best thing for her, had taken its toll. She'd been moody and pissy and okay, she was big to admit it, a bit dramatic.

Hey, she was her mother's daughter.

But none of that explained why the man of her dreams was going to break her heart.

Another deep breath did little to help, but it would have to do. Between helping her sister plan tonight's party and Josh's strange behavior, Melissa knew she was holding herself together with the thinnest of threads.

The scent of fresh coffee drifted through the house and Melissa groaned. Oh, how she ached for a hot cup, swimming in cream and lots of sugar.

Pushing the thought from her head, she picked up the gift basket that held everything her parents would need for a perfect second honeymoon in Italy. There was a small alcove right next to the dining room, a perfect place to stash it until just the right moment.

Turning, she headed for the door of her sister's office when the matching antique photo frames on a nearby bookshelf caught her eye.

The one on the right, taken just a few short years ago, was of Abby and Greg standing at the altar just after being presented to their friends and family as Mr. and Mrs. Gregory DeSena. Despite the elaborate setting, and the huge bridal party standing other either side of them, Melissa right there next to her sister, Abby and Greg only had eyes for each other. In fact, the photographer had captured the picture just as Greg had gently wiped a tear from her sister's cheek.

The other photograph, a bit more formal in mono-chrome colors of black and white, showed her mother and father on their wedding day. Her mother looked so young, so beautiful, so thin. Daddy was as hand-some as ever in his tuxedo, his arm around his bride, his hand easily spanning her waist. The bridal bouquet was larger and over-the-top, typical for the early 80's, but her mother's dress…

Melissa squeezed tighter to the basket, the cello-phane crinkling loudly in the silent room.

Abby had planned her wedding with the precision of an army general, right down to her chiffon, A-line sil-houette gown with just enough crystal bling along the shoulder straps to give a special sparkle. Their mother looked the opposite, but just as beautiful wearing her own mother's gown, a vintage 1960 beauty of satin, lace and tulle with a circular skirt that cried out for layers of crinoline, a square-neck bodice and sleeves that hugged her arms.

A dress that Melissa had always seen herself wear-ing one day.

The day she married Josh.

Of course, she'd change into something short and sexy and perfect for dancing the night away after the ceremony, but—

"Oh, what does it matter!" Melissa said aloud. "It's not going to happen! It's never going to happen. Josh doesn't want to date you anymore, much less even think about getting down on one knee."

She exited the room and hurried down the long hall, tucking the basket just out of sight. They would have dessert, present the gift and then she would find a way to get Josh to take her home as soon as possible.

For the last time.

This was all Greg's fault.

As heartbreaking as it was, because she and Frank had always loved Greg, Diana knew deep in her heart that the man they'd welcomed in their home, into their hearts, was on the verge of walking out on their daughter.

How could Greg do this to Abby?

They were perfect together, complemented each other so well because they were so alike. Levelheaded, organized to a fault, methodical even.

Diana paused and grabbed hold of the stairway landing.

Could that be it?

Could Abby and Greg be too much alike? Had her son-in-law found someone else? Someone cute and bubbly who hung on his every word like it was gold?

Abby had mentioned a coworker of Greg's they'd run into one night while out to dinner. She'd said he'd been reluctant to introduce them, which seemed strange as the woman had literally gushed at how much she enjoyed working with Abby's husband when she'd stopped by their table.

The need to get to Frank, to squeeze his hand and have him comfort her, rolled over Diana. She needed him to tell her that everything would be all right, that she'd been right all along, and promise her they'd fight tooth and nail for their daughter so she didn't lose this beautiful home.

"Mom?"

Diana looked up and found Melissa standing there.

"Are you okay?" Melissa asked. "You look a little pale."

"I'm fine."

"You've got a death grip on the railing."

Diana immediately released her hold. "I just got a bit light-headed for a moment."

Concern filled her daughter's beautiful eyes. She motioned to the steps that led to the second floor. "Here, let's sit."

"But your sister is—"

"Perfectly capable of pulling dessert together all on her own," Melissa took her arm and the two of them sat. "Disgustingly capable, as we both know."

Diana sat, basically because she had no choice, taking the time to really look at her daughter. She'd been crying. Her baby suffered the same fate as she did when tears came—puffy eyes. And while Melissa had been acting strange during dinner, this was the first true evidence Diana had that something was terribly wrong.

"Darling, you seem a bit…off this evening." Diana kept her tone light after a few minutes of silence passed. "How is everything with you? You didn't eat very much tonight."

Melissa stared at her clenched hands. "Everything is just fine, mother. It's been a long week and I'm very tired."

"Yes, you said you've been working long hours. That's probably cut into your free time with Josh."

"Y-yes, it has, but I don't think that's going to be a problem much longer."

"What does that mean?"

Melissa rose, one hand pressed against her stomach. "It's nothing. You were right. We should get back into the dining room. You know how Abby gets when things go off schedule."

Yes, she did know. Oh, the divorce was going to upset Abby's tidy world, but that didn't mean that Diana wouldn't be there for her other daughter, as well. She still had no idea what was bothering her youngest, but she would find out before this evening was through.

And she would make things right.

For both her girls.

She'd easily found the time to attend Abby's debates, girl scout meetings and band concerts and never missed a dance recital, theatre production or football game while Melissa was on the cheerleading squad. Her daughters might be grown, but they still needed their mother.

Now more than ever.

Diana stood, as well. "Yes, let's go back and join everyone."

They walked into the room and Diana's gaze locked with Frank's. Her husband watched her every step as she moved around the table to retake her seat next to him. Thirty years of marriage honed his deduction skills to a razor-sharp point, and she knew that he knew she'd found out something.

"Okay, let's get this celebration going." Greg spoke from where he stood at the buffet filling tall fluted glasses with sparkling liquid, having already popped open the bottle. "Josh, why don't you hand out the champagne to everyone?"

Frank leaned in close. "What's wrong?"

Diana batted her eyes, determined not to cry as his gentle and caring tone was sure to bring on the waterworks. "Not now, darling."

"So you were worried for nothing?"

"Of course not. I was right all along—" She cut off her words when Abby came in with a tray of desserts in her hands. "Dear, can I help with those?"

"No, you stay seated, Mom. It'll only take me a moment to hand these out."

True to her words, the etched-crystal parfait dishes were soon at everyone's place setting and, immediately after, Josh placed a glass in front of Frank and Diana.

Diana watched as he then went back to get two more for Greg and Abby and one last trip for the final two glasses.

"Here you go, sweetheart." He moved in behind Melissa and reached past her shoulder to place a glass in front of her.

"No, thank you." Her baby girl's voice was strained.

"You don't want any champagne?" Josh was clearly confused. "You love the stuff. We practically finished off a magnum ourselves last New Year's Eve."

Melissa shook her head, her dark locks flying over her shoulder. "I'm sure. I'll just h-have—" She paused, pressing her fingertips to her mouth for a quick moment. "I'd prefer a cup of coffee. Decaf, please."

Oh, everything made sense now!

The tears, the exhaustion, the hand held protectively over her still flat belly, the refusal of alcohol. Her motherly intrusion might have been late in picking up on Melissa's distress, but the realization over what her baby was facing hit Diana like a thunderbolt coming from the sky.

Her heart didn't know whether to break for the certain pain Abby was facing over the end of her marriage or rejoice with the news that she was finally going to be a grandmother!

Her baby was having a baby!

Chapter Five
by Gina Wilkins

During the year he and Melissa Morgan had been together, Josh Wright thought he'd come to know her family fairly well, but there were still times when he felt like an outsider who couldn't quite catch on to the family rhythms. Tonight was one of those occasions.

The undercurrents of tension at the elegantly set dinner table were obvious enough, even to him.

Melissa had been acting oddly all evening. Abby and Greg kept exchanging significant looks, as though messages passed between them that no one else could hear. Even Melissa and Abby's mom, Diana, typically the life of any dinner party, was unnaturally subdued and introspective tonight. Only the family patriarch, Frank, seemed as steady and unruffled as ever, characteristically enjoying the time with his family without getting drawn in to their occasional, usually Diana-generated melodramas.

Josh didn't have a clue what was going on with any of them. Shouldn't he understand them better by now, considering he wanted so badly to be truly one of them soon?

He dipped his spoon into the dessert dish in front of him, scooping up a bite of fresh raspberries, an orange-liqueur flavored mascarpone cheese mixture and ladyfingers spread with what tasted like raspberry jam. "Abby, this dessert is amazing."

She smiled across the table at him. "Thank you. Mom and Dad had tiramisu the first night of their honeymoon, so I tried to recreate that nice memory."

"Ours wasn't flavored with orange and raspberry," Diana seemed compelled to point out. "We had a more traditional espresso-based tiramisu."

Abby's smile turned just a bit wry. "I found this recipe online and thought it sounded good. I wasn't trying to exactly reproduce what you had before, Mom."

"I think this one is even better," Frank interjected hastily, after swallowing a big bite of his dessert. "Who'd have thought thirty years later we'd be eating tiramisu made by our own little girl, eh, Diana?"

Everyone smiled—except Melissa, who was playing with her dessert without her usual enthusiasm for sweets. It bothered Josh that Melissa seemed to become more withdrawn and somber as the evening progressed. Though she had made a noticeable effort to participate in the dining table conversation, her eyes were darkened to almost jade and the few smiles she'd managed looked forced. As well as he knew her, as much as he loved her, he sensed when she was stressed or unhappy. For some reason, she seemed both tonight, and that was twisting him into knots.

Maybe Abby had been right when she'd warned him that his nervous anticipation was affecting Melissa, though he thought he'd done a better job of hiding it from her. Apparently, she knew him a bit too well, also.

Encouraged by the response to his compliment of the dessert, he thought he would try again to keep the conversation light and cheerful. Maybe Melissa would relax if everyone else did.

Mindful of the reason for this gathering—and because he was rather obsessed with love and marriage, anyway—he said, "Thirty years. That's a remarkable accomplishment these days. Not many couples are able to keep the fire alive for that long."

He couldn't imagine his passion for Melissa ever burning out, not in thirty years—or fifty, for that matter.

He felt her shift in her seat next to him and her spoon clicked against her dessert dish. He glanced sideways at her, but she was looking down at her dish, her glossy black hair falling forward to hide her face from him.

Frank, at least, seemed pleased with Josh's observation.

"That's it, exactly." Frank pointed his spoon in Josh's direction, almost dripping raspberry jam on the tablecloth. "Keeping the fire alive. Takes work, but it's worth it, right, hon?"

"Absolutely." Diana looked hard at Abby and Greg as she spoke. "All marriages go through challenging times, but with love and patience and mutual effort, the rewards will come."

Abby and Greg shared a startled look, but Frank spoke again before either of them could respond to what seemed like a sermon aimed directly at them. "I still remember the day I met her, just like it was yesterday."

That sounded like a story worth pursuing. Though everyone else had probably heard it many times, Josh encouraged Frank to continue. "I'd like to hear about it. How did you meet?"

Frank's smile was nostalgic, his eyes distant with the memories. "I was the best man in a college friend's wedding. Diana was the maid of honor. I had a flat tire on the way to the wedding rehearsal, so I was late arriving."

Diana shook her head. Though she still looked worried about something, she was paying attention to her husband's tale. "The bride was fit to be tied that it looked as though the best man wasn't going to show up for the rehearsal. She was a nervous wreck, even though her groom kept assuring her Frank could be counted on to be there."

Frank chuckled. "Anyway, the minute I arrived, all rumpled and dusty from changing the tire, I was rushed straight to a little room off the church sanctuary where the groom's party was gathered getting ready to enter on cue. I didn't have a chance to socialize or meet the other wedding party members before the rehearsal began. Five minutes after I dashed in, I was standing at the front of the church next to my friend Jim. And then the music began and the bridesmaids started their march in. Diana was the third bridesmaid to enter."

"Gretchen was first, Bridget next."

Ignoring the details Diana inserted, Frank continued, "She was wearing a green dress, the same color as her eyes. The minute she walked into the church, I felt my heart flop like a landed fish."

Diana laughed ruefully. "Well, that doesn't sound very romantic."

Frank patted her hand, still lost in his memories. "She stopped halfway down the aisle and informed the organist that she was playing much too slowly and that everyone in the audience would fall asleep before the whole wedding party reached the front of the church."

"Well, she was."

Frank chuckled and winked at Josh. "That was when I knew this was someone I had to meet."

Charmed by the story, Josh remembered the first moment he'd laid eyes on Melissa. He understood that "floppy fish" analogy all too well, though he'd compared his own heart to a runaway train. He could still recall how hard it had raced when Melissa had tossed back her dark hair and laughed up at him for the first time, her green eyes sparkling with humor and warmth. He'd actually wondered for a moment if she could hear it pounding against his chest.

"So it was love at first sight?"

Frank nodded decisively. "That it was."

"And when did you know she was 'the one' for you? That you wanted to marry her?"

"Probably right then. But certainly the next evening during the ceremony, after I'd spent a few hours getting to know Diana. When I found myself mentally saying 'I do' when the preacher asked 'Do you take this woman?' I knew I was hooked."

Josh sighed. This, he thought, was why he wanted to wait for the absolute perfect moment to propose to Melissa. Someday he hoped to tell a story that would make everyone who heard it say "Awww," the way he felt like doing now. "You're a lucky man, Frank. Not every guy is fortunate enough to find a woman he wants to spend the rest of his life with."

Three lucky men sat at this table tonight, he thought happily. Like Frank and Greg, he had found his perfect match.

Melissa dropped her spoon with a clatter and sprang to her feet. "I, uh— Excuse me," she muttered, her voice choked. "I'm not feeling well."

Before Josh or anyone else could ask her what was wrong, she dashed from the room. Concerned, he half rose from his seat, intending to follow her.

"What on earth is wrong with Melissa?" Frank asked in bewilderment.

Words burst from Diana as if she'd held them in as long as she was physically able. "Melissa is pregnant."

His knees turning to gelatin, Josh fell back into his chair with a thump.

After patting her face with a towel, Melissa looked in the bathroom mirror to make sure she'd removed all signs of her bout of tears. She was quite sure Abby would say she was overreacting and being overly dramatic—just like their Mom, Abby would say with a shake of her auburn head—but Melissa couldn't help it. Every time she thought about her life without Josh in it tears welled up behind her eyes and it was all she could do to keep them from gushing out.

Abby had tried to convince her she was only imagining that Josh was trying to find a way to break up with her. As much as she wanted to believe her sister, Melissa was convinced her qualms were well-founded. She knew every expression that crossed Josh's handsome face. Every flicker of emotion that passed through his clear blue eyes. He had grown increasingly nervous and awkward around her during the past few days, when they had always been so close, so connected, so easy together before. Passion was only a part of their relationship—though certainly a major part. But the mental connection between them was even more special—or at least it had been.

She didn't know what had gone wrong. Everything had seemed so perfect until Josh's behavior had suddenly changed. But maybe the questions he had asked her dad tonight had been a clue. Maybe he had concluded that he didn't really want to spend the rest of his life with her. That only a few men were lucky enough to find "the one."

She had so hoped she was Josh's "one."

Feeling tears threaten again, she drew a deep breath and lifted her chin, ordering herself to reclaim her pride. She would survive losing Josh, she assured herself. Maybe.

Forcing herself to leave Abby's guest bathroom, she headed for the dining room, expecting to hear conversation and the clinking of silverware and china. Instead what appeared to be stunned silence gripped the five people sitting at the table. Her gaze went instinctively to Josh, finding him staring back at her. His dark blond hair tumbled almost into his eyes, making him look oddly disheveled and perturbed. She realized suddenly that everyone else was gawking at her, too. Did she see sympathy on her father's face?

Before she could stop herself, she leaped to a stomach-wrenching conclusion. Had Josh told her family that he was breaking up with her? Is that why they were all looking at her like…well, like that?

"What?" she asked apprehensively.

"Why didn't you tell me?" Josh demanded.

It occurred to her that he sounded incongruously hurt, considering he was the one on the verge of breaking her heart. "Tell you what?"

"That you're pregnant."

"I'm—?" Her voice shot up into a squeak of surprise, unable to complete the sentence.

"Don't worry, darling, we'll all be here for you," Diana assured her, wiping her eyes with the corner of a napkin. "Just as we'll be here for you, Abby, after you and Greg split up. Although I sincerely hope you'll try to work everything out before you go your separate ways."

"Wait. What?" Greg's chair scraped against the floor as he spun to stare at his wife. "What is she talking about, Abby?"

Melissa felt as if she'd left a calm, orderly dinner party and returned only minutes later to sheer pandemonium.

"What on earth makes you think I'm pregnant?" she asked Josh, unable to concentrate on her sister's sputtering at the moment.

He looked from her to her mom and back again, growing visibly more confused by the minute. "Your mother told us."

Her mother sighed and nodded. "I've overheard a few snippets of conversation today. Enough to put two and two together about what's going on with both my poor girls. You're giving up caffeine and you're feeling queasy and we've all noticed that you've been upset all evening."

"Mom, I don't know what you heard—" Abby began, but Melissa talked over her sister.

"You're completely off base, Mom," she said firmly, avoiding Josh's eyes until she was sure she could look at him without succumbing to those looming tears again. "I'm giving up caffeine because I think I've been drinking too much of it for my health. I'm not pregnant."

Regret swept through her with the words. Maybe she was being overly dramatic again, but the thought of never having a child with Josh almost sent her bolting for the bathroom with another bout of hot tears.

She risked a quick glance at him, but she couldn't quite read his expression. He sat silently in his chair, his expression completely inscrutable now. She assumed he was deeply relieved to find out she wasn't pregnant, but the relief wasn't evident on his face. Maybe he was thinking about what a close call he'd just escaped.

Her mom searched her face. "You're not?"

Melissa shook her head. "No. I'm not."

"Then why have you been so upset this evening?"

Rattled by this entire confrontation, she blurted, "I'm upset because Josh is breaking up with me."

Josh made a choked sound before pushing a hand

through his hair in exasperation. "Why do you think I'm breaking up with you?"

"I just, um, put two and two together," she muttered, all too aware that she sounded as much like her mother as Abby always accused her.

"Well, then you need to work on your math skills," Josh shot back with a frustrated shake of his head. "I don't want to break up with you, Melissa. I want to ask you to marry me!"

Chapter Six
by Cindy Kirk

Bedlam followed Josh Wright's announcement that he planned to propose to Melissa Morgan. Everyone at the table started talking in loud excited voices, their hands gesturing wildly.

Family patriarch Frank Morgan had experience with chaotic situations. After all, he and his wife Diana had raised two girls. When things got out of hand, control had to be established. Because his silver referee whistle was in a drawer back home, Frank improvised.

Seconds later, a shrill noise split the air.

His family immediately stopped talking and all turned in his direction.

"Frank?" Shock blanketed Greg DeSena's face. Though he'd been married to Frank's oldest daughter, Abby, for three years, this was a side to his father-in-law he'd obviously never seen.

Frank's youngest daughter, Melissa, slipped into her chair without being asked. She cast furtive glances at her boyfriend, Josh. It had been Josh's unexpected proclamation that he intended to propose to her that had thrown everyone into such a tizzy.

Even though Frank hadn't whistled a family meeting to order in years, his wife and daughters remembered what the blast of air meant.

"Darling." Diana spoke in a low tone, but loud enough for everyone at the table to hear clearly. "This is our anniversary dinner. Can't a family meeting wait until another time?"

Her green eyes looked liked liquid jade in the candlelight. Even after thirty years, one look from her, one touch, was all it took to make Frank fall in love all over again.

If they were at their home—instead of at Greg and Abby's house—he'd grab her hand and they'd trip up the stairs, kissing and shedding clothes with every step. But he was the head of this warm, wonderful, sometimes crazy family and with the position came responsibility.

"I'm sorry, sweetheart. This can't wait." Frank shifted his gaze from his beautiful wife and settled it on the man who'd blurted out his intentions only moments before. "Josh."

His future son-in-law snapped to attention. "Sir."

Though Frank hadn't been a marine in a very long time, Josh's response showed he'd retained his commanding presence. "Sounds like there's something you want to ask my daughter."

"Frank, no. Not now," Diana protested. "Not like this."

"Mr. Morgan is right." Josh pushed back his chair and stood. "There *is* something I want to ask Melissa. From the misunderstanding tonight, it appears I've already waited too long."

Frank nodded approvingly and sat back in his chair. He liked a decisive man. Josh would be a good addition to the family.

"If you want to wait—" Diana began.

Before she could finish, Frank leaned over and did what he'd wanted to do all night. He kissed her.

"Let the man say his piece," he murmured against her lips.

Diana shuddered. Her breathing hitched but predictably she opened her mouth. So he kissed her again. This time deeper, longer, until her eyes lost their focus, until she relaxed against his shoulder with a happy sigh.

Josh held out his hand to Melissa. His heart pounded so hard against his ribs, he felt almost faint. But he was going to do it. Now. Finally.

With a tremulous smile, Melissa placed her slender fingers in his. The lines that had furrowed her pretty brow the past couple of weeks disappeared. His heart clenched as he realized he'd been to blame for her distress. Well, he wouldn't delay a second longer. He promptly dropped to one knee.

"Melissa," Josh began then stopped when his voice broke. He glanced around the table. All eyes were on him, but no one dared to speak. Abby and Greg offered encouraging smiles. His future in-laws nodded approvingly.

His girlfriend's eyes never left his face. The love he saw shining in the emerald depths gave him courage to continue.

"When I first saw you at the office Christmas party, I was struck by your beauty. It wasn't until we began dating that I realized you are as beautiful inside as out."

Melissa blinked back tears. Josh hoped they were tears of happiness.

"This past year I've fallen deeper and deeper in love with you. I can't imagine my life without you in it. I want your face to be the last I see at night and the first I see every morning. I want to have children with you. I want to grow old with you. I promise I'll do everything in my power to make you happy."

He was rambling. Speaking from the heart to be sure, but rambling. For a second Josh wished he had the speech he'd tinkered with over the past couple of months with him now, the one with the pretty words and poetic phrases. But it was across the room in his jacket pocket and too late to be of help now.

Josh slipped a small box from his pocket and snapped open the lid. The diamond he'd seen circled in her bride's magazine was nestled inside. The large stone caught the light and sparkled with an impressive brilliance. "I love you more than I thought it was possible to love someone."

He'd told himself he wasn't going to say another word but surely a declaration of such magnitude couldn't be considered rambling.

Her lips curved upward and she expelled a happy sigh. "I love you, too."

Josh resisted the urge to jump to his feet and do a little

home-plate dance. He reminded himself there would be plenty of time for celebration once the ring was on her finger.

With great care, Josh lifted the diamond from the black velvet. He was primed to slip it on when she pulled her hand back ever-so-slightly.

"Isn't there something you want to ask me?" Melissa whispered.

At first Josh couldn't figure out what she was referring to until he realized with sudden horror that he hadn't actually popped the question. Heat rose up his neck. Thankfully he was still on one knee. "Melissa, will you make me the happiest man in the world and marry me?"

The words came out in one breath and were a bit garbled, but she didn't appear to notice.

"Yes. Oh, yes."

Relief flooded him. He slid the ring in place with trembling fingers. "If you don't like it we can—"

"It's perfect. Absolutely perfect." Tears slipped down her cheeks.

He stood and pulled her close, kissing her soundly. "I wanted this to be special—"

"It is special." Melissa turned toward her family and smiled through happy tears. "I can't imagine anything better than having my family here to celebrate with us."

"This calls for a toast." Flashing a smile that was almost as bright as his daughter's, Frank picked up the nearest bottle of champagne. He filled Diana's glass and then his own before passing the bottle around the table.

Greg filled his glass and those of Josh and Melissa's

but Abby, his wife, covered her glass with her hand and shook her head.

Frank stood and raised his glass high. "To Josh and Melissa. May you be as happy together as Diana and I have been for the past thirty years."

Words of congratulations and the sound of clinking glasses filled the air.

Nestled in the crook of her future husband's arm, Melissa giggled. Normally her mom knew everything before everyone else. Not this time.

"You thought I was pregnant because I wanted decaf coffee," she said to her mother, "but yet you don't find it odd that Abby hasn't had a sip of alcohol tonight?"

For a woman like Diana who prided herself on being in the "know," the comment was tantamount to waving a red flag in front of a bull. She whirled and fixed her gaze on her firstborn, who stood with her head resting against her husband's shoulder. "Honey, is there something you and Greg want to tell us?"

Abby's cheeks pinked. She straightened and exchanged a look with her husband. He gave a slight nod. She took one breath. And then another. "Greg and I, well, we're...we're pregnant."

"A baby!" Diana shrieked and moved so suddenly she'd have upset her glass of champagne, if Frank hadn't grabbed it. "I can't believe it. Our two girls, all grown up. One getting married. One having a baby. This is truly a happy day."

Everyone seemed to agree as tears of joy flowed as freely as the champagne, accompanied by much back-slapping.

"Have you thought of any names?" Diana asked

Abby and Greg then turned to Melissa and Josh. "Any idea on a wedding date?"

Suggestions on both came fast and furious until Abby realized the party had gotten off track. She pulled her sister aside. "The anniversary gift," she said in a low tone to Melissa. "We need to give them their gift."

"I'll get it." In a matter of seconds, Melissa returned, cradling the large basket in her arms.

Josh moved to her side, as if he couldn't bear to be far from his new fiancée. Greg stood behind his wife, his arms around her still slender waist.

"Mom and Dad," Melissa began. "You've shown us what love looks like."

"What it feels like," Abby added.

With a flourish, Melissa presented her parents with a basket overflowing with biscotti, gourmet cappuccino mix, and other items reminiscent of their honeymoon in Italy…along with assorted travel documents. "Congratulations on thirty years of marriage."

"And best wishes for thirty more," Abby and Melissa said in unison, with Josh and Greg chiming in.

"Oh, Frank, isn't this the best evening ever?" Diana's voice bubbled with excitement. "All this good news and gifts, too."

She exclaimed over every item in the basket but grew silent when she got to the tickets, guidebooks and brochures. Diana glanced at her husband. He shrugged, looking equally puzzled.

"It's a trip," Abby explained.

Melissa smiled. "We've booked you on a four-star vacation to Italy, so you can recreate your honeymoon, only this time in comfort and style."

"Oh, my stars." Diana put a hand to her head. When she began to sway, her husband slipped a steadying arm around her shoulders.

"I think your mom has had a bit too much excitement for one day." Frank chuckled. "Or maybe a little too much of the vino."

"I've only had two glasses. Or was it three?" Instead of elbowing him in the side as he expected, she laughed and refocused on her children. "Regardless, thank you all for such wonderful, thoughtful presents."

Abby exchanged a relieved glance with Melissa. "We wanted to give you and Dad the perfect gift to celebrate your years of happiness together."

"You already have," Frank said, his voice thick with emotion.

He shifted his gaze from Abby and Greg to Melissa and Josh before letting it linger on his beautiful wife, Diana. A wedding in the spring. A grandbaby next summer. A wonderful woman to share his days and nights. Who could ask for more?

* * * * *

HEART & HOME

Heartwarming romances where love can
happen right when you least expect it.

♦ Harlequin®
SPECIAL EDITION®

COMING NEXT MONTH
AVAILABLE APRIL 24, 2012

You can find more information on upcoming Harlequin® titles,
free excerpts and more at www.HarlequinInsideRomance.com.

HSECNM0412

REQUEST YOUR FREE BOOKS!

2 FREE NOVELS PLUS 2 FREE GIFTS!

❧ Harlequin®

SPECIAL EDITION

Life, Love & Family

YES! Please send me 2 FREE Harlequin® Special Edition novels and my 2 FREE gifts (gifts are worth about $10). After receiving them, if I don't wish to receive any more books, I can return the shipping statement marked "cancel." If I don't cancel, I will receive 6 brand-new novels every month and be billed just $4.49 per book in the U.S. or $5.24 per book in Canada. That's a saving of at least 14% off the cover price! It's quite a bargain! Shipping and handling is just 50¢ per book in the U.S. and 75¢ per book in Canada.* I understand that accepting the 2 free books and gifts places me under no obligation to buy anything. I can always return a shipment and cancel at any time. Even if I never buy another book, the two free books and gifts are mine to keep forever.

235/335 HDN FEGF

Name	(PLEASE PRINT)
Address	Apt. #
City	State/Prov.	Zip/Postal Code

Signature (if under 18, a parent or guardian must sign)

Mail to the **Reader Service:**
IN U.S.A.: P.O. Box 1867, Buffalo, NY 14240-1867
IN CANADA: P.O. Box 609, Fort Erie, Ontario L2A 5X3

Not valid for current subscribers to Harlequin Special Edition books.

Want to try two free books from another line?
Call 1-800-873-8635 or visit www.ReaderService.com.

* Terms and prices subject to change without notice. Prices do not include applicable taxes. Sales tax applicable in N.Y. Canadian residents will be charged applicable taxes. Offer not valid in Quebec. This offer is limited to one order per household. All orders subject to credit approval. Credit or debit balances in a customer's account(s) may be offset by any other outstanding balance owed by or to the customer. Please allow 4 to 6 weeks for delivery. Offer available while quantities last.

Your Privacy—The Reader Service is committed to protecting your privacy. Our Privacy Policy is available online at www.ReaderService.com or upon request from the Reader Service.

We make a portion of our mailing list available to reputable third parties that offer products we believe may interest you. If you prefer that we not exchange your name with third parties, or if you wish to clarify or modify your communication preferences, please visit us at www.ReaderService.com/consumerchoice or write to us at Reader Service Preference Service, P.O. Box 9062, Buffalo, NY 14269. Include your complete name and address.

HSE11B

Harlequin®

American ★ *Romance*®

The heartwarming conclusion of

from fan-favorite author
TINA LEONARD

With five brothers married, Jonas Callahan is under no
pressure to tie the knot. But when Sabrina McKinley
admits her bouncing baby boy is his, Jonas does
everything he can to win over the woman he's loved
for years. First the last Callahan bachelor must uncover
an important family secret...before he can take
the lovely Sabrina down the aisle!

A Callahan Wedding

**Available this May
wherever books are sold.**

www.Harlequin.com

HAR75405

*After a bad decision—or two—Annie Mendes
is determined to succeed as a P.I. But her first assignment
could be her last, because one thing is clear: she's not cut
out to be a nanny. And Louisiana detective Nate Dufrene
seems to know there's more to her than meets the eye!*

*Read on for an exciting excerpt of the upcoming book
WATERS RUN DEEP by Liz Talley...*

THE SOUND OF A CAR behind her had Annie scooting off the road and checking over her shoulder.

Nate Dufrene.

Her heart took on a galloping rhythm that had nothing to do with exercise.

He slowed beside her. "Wanna ride?"

"I'm almost there. Besides, I wouldn't want to get your seat sweaty."

His gaze traveled down her body before meeting her eyes. Awareness ignited in her blood. "I don't mind."

Her mind screamed, *get your butt back to the house and leave Nate alone.* Her libido, however, told her to take the candy he offered and climb into his car like a naughty little girl. Damn, it was hard to ignore candy like him.

"If you don't mind." She pulled open the door and climbed inside.

The slight scent of citrus cologne, which suited him, filled the car. She inhaled, sucking in cool air and Nate. Both were good.

"You run often?" he asked.

"Three or four times a week."

"Oh, yeah? Maybe we can go for a run together."

Her body tightened unwillingly as thoughts of other things they could do together flitted through her mind. She shrugged as though his presence wasn't affecting her. Which it *so* was. Lord, what was wrong with her? *He* wasn't her assignment.

"Sure." No way—not if she wanted to keep her job. As he parked, she reached for the door handle, but his hand on her arm stopped her. His touch was warm, even on her heated flesh.

"What did you say you were before becoming a nanny?"

Alarm choked out the weird sexual energy that had been humming in her for the past few minutes. Maybe meeting him on the road wasn't as coincidental as it first seemed. "A real-estate agent."

Will Nate discover Annie's secret?
Find out in WATERS RUN DEEP by Liz Talley,
available May 2012 from Harlequin® Superromance®.

And be sure to look for the other two books
in Liz's THE BOYS OF BAYOU BRIDGE series,
available in July and September 2012.

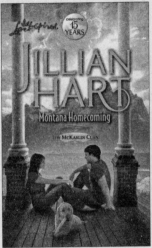

Love Inspired

Hoping to shield
the secret she carries,
Brooke McKaslin returns
to Montana on family
business. She's not
planning on staying
long—until she begins
working for reporter
Liam Knightly. Liam is
as leery of relationships
as Brooke but as their
romance develops, Brooke
worries that her secret may
ruin any chance at love.

Montana Homecoming

By fan-favorite author

JILLIAN HART

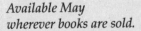

THE McKASLIN CLAN